MW00770618

Asiri and the Amaru

Copyright © 2023 by Natalia Hernandez

All rights reserved.

This is a work of fiction. All character and events portrayed in this novel are fictitious. Any resemblance to real people of events is purely coincidental.

TITLE: Asiri and the Amaru

AUTHOR: Natalia Hernandez

ON-SALE DATE: OCTOBER 24, 2023

Paperback ISBN: 979-8-9865983-6-9

Ebook ISBN: 979-8-9865983-7-6

Book Cover Design by: ebooklaunch.com

Chapter Illustrations by Natalia Hernandez

Chapter Heading Images by Mikhail Seleznev

Developmental Edits by: My'Kayle Pugh

Copy Edits by: Ashley Wessel

For more information, please visit:

www.NataliaHernandezAuthor.com

No portion of this book may be reproduced in any form without written permission from the publisher or author, except as permitted by U.S. copyright law.

NATALIA
HERNANDEZ

ASIRI AND THE AMARU

For my mother, who taught me so much about my ancestors and
my culture.
Gracias.

...

(Just don't read Chapter 17. Or 19.
Or ... you know what? I'll send you your own copy!)

Content Warnings

This is an adult fantasy novel and contains romantic and sexual interactions between consenting (and enthusiastic!) adults. Please read responsibly.

Additional content warnings include:

- Injured animals (<u>NO animal cruelty and NO animals die in this book</u>—except for some fish which are eaten by another animal, and a few insects. Non-graphic.)

- Magic/supernatural abilities

- Earthquakes (No deaths occur)

- Tsunami (No deaths occur)

CONTENTS

SOUTH AMERICAN CORAL SNAKE/ NACA-NACA

Chapter 1

Asiri

Assembling a condor, a cougar, and a snake in a singular location was a complicated endeavor on a good day.

The task was infinitely more difficult, however, when the three happened to hate one other.

Kuntur, the condor, remained convinced that—given the first opportunity—Puma the cougar would eat him. Which was, of course, just what Katari the serpent feared that Kuntur would do to her.

And most bizarre of all, Puma feared that Katari would spring up and pierce the paws of the large cat with a toxic venom at the first provocation, despite the fact that Katari had expressly stated several times that *she was not venomous.*[1]

It could all turn into quite a mess if one wasn't careful.

Luckily, Asiri was very, *very* good at her job. It was a wonder that Casa de Murmuros was allowing her to leave their service;

---

1. This is, of course, a bold-faced lie. South American coral snakes are most assuredly venomous. But Puma needn't know that.

Creature Communing was so rare an ability. And Asiri was the most gifted Communer of their age.

Regardless, this would be the last time she assembled the sacred three to hear and interpret the whispered warnings of the universe. Asiri's father and head shaman of the Casa, Kallpa Yupanqui, had agreed: one more mission, one more message, and Asiri would no longer be at the beck and call of the Casa or their clients.[2] She could live her own life, be her own person.

If only she could get through this final Communion.

"Amiges," she respectfully started, but before she could get any further, Kuntur interrupted her.[3]

He let out a loud, chittering screech, chuffing quick bursts of air through his curved beak.

"They're getting closer to me, Asiri!" he belted out. The condor's voice was high and surprisingly melodious, especially when compared to the rumbling calls of alarm he had broken the relative silence of the forest with.

Asiri knew from experience that to anyone else listening, Kuntur would sound as if he was just hissing and grunting like any other condor would. They wouldn't understand the words of the bird, and should they catch Asiri speaking to him, they were more likely to assume that she was mad rather than a Creature Communer.

---

2. "Yupanqui" is a Quechua surname conveying a title of distinction. The name Yupanqui means "with honor." This can be comparable to "The Honorable Kallpa."

3. "Amige" is a gender-neutral word for "friend."

Most everyday people had little to no knowledge of the gifts and talents which were housed in Casa de Murmuros. Some didn't even believe that a person who could understand and speak to animals truly existed. Even for the ones who trusted in the Casa's power, a woman who could Commune with creatures was a bit hard to believe. Despite this, many people visited the house of secrets, seeking answers to questions that only the Casa could provide.

For the right price, of course.

But Asiri didn't have to worry about anyone catching her speaking to the animals today. A three-day hike up the perilous slopes of the Andean mountains to find her animal guides left her far from the people of her village. The air was thin with the elevation, but the view of the vast sprawling mountains with their soft verdant bedding of plants, trees, vines, and moss made the wearying trip worthwhile.

Katari was curled up in a loose coil on top of a sloped, ruddy rock near the mountain's unshaded precipice. Her scaled, sinuous body was ringed with bold swatches of intermittent red and black which were currently soaking up the midday rays. As she basked in the warmth, her head swayed from side to side in undulating movements, her pink tongue darting out from time to time.

Kuntur perched on the low branch of a Palo Santo tree, his feathers ruffled and sticking out at jagged angles, some bunched up around his neck like a winter coat. His impressive beak clicked together as he pointedly glared at the cougar.

Puma, despite Kuntur's accusations, was not inching their way towards the condor, but sprawled out languidly under the shade of a neighboring tree. Although their body was deliberately nonchalant, their golden eyes continuously flicked towards Katari, claws flexing each time they dared a peak.

Asiri fought the urge to rub her temples.

It was like this every time she had to assemble the sacred three. Luckily, most questions that came to the Casa did not need the aid of such illustrious guides. Most requests were mundane, even petty. If the ruler of a farming community wanted to know why their crops were failing in a particular year, Asiri could ask the nearby crows or field mice if they had noticed anything amiss, such as an excess of insects or negligent farmers.

Political rivals across borders could request macaws to act as spies and survey enemy troops from overhead, or palace rats to collect information heard through walls or underneath floor-boards.

Or—as on one rare occasion—if there was no human in a household to witness a death, but the deceased had a cat, infor-mation could easily be gathered.

But some questions were just too big, too important to be answered in this realm alone. Some needed the connection to all three realms, and the whispered warnings of the universe itself, which could only come with pure alignment.

Which is why she needed her three animal guides.

Kuntur, as the noble soarer, had a direct connection to Hanan Pacha, the realm of the dioses above.[4]

---

4. The word "pacha" is often translated into "world," however, it is more accurate to say "realm" or "plane of existence."

Puma was a representative of Kay Pacha, the realm in which most living creatures reside and where humans and so many other beings dwell.

And finally, Katari had access to Ukhu Pacha, the realm of not only the dead but also of new life.

Asiri knew the realms did not exist in separate spaces, but instead occupied the same space and time, layered above one another, and interlaced in an endless connection of being. The veils between each realm shifted and stretched but were a challenge to traverse.. The only way to do so was to gather each of their earthly representatives and attempt to pierce all three at once, dwelling momentarily in the space between. Only there could she find the answers she sought.

She just had to get the three creatures to work together once again.

"Puma," she addressed the large cat, angling her head down in respect. "Could you tell Kuntur that you promise not to try to eat him, por favor?"

Puma's gaze finally snapped back from Katari, pinning Kuntur under their watch instead. Their body visibly relaxed, and their mouth opened in a large, canine-flashing yawn, making the bird squawk and jump further up his branch.

When Puma's enormous jaw finally snapped back shut, Asiri had to suppress a wince at the grinding sound of sharp teeth grating against one another.

"That wiry bundle of gristle isn't even worth the mouthful," they murmured lazily, stretching their paws in front of them to flex and retract their claws.

"Still," Puma wondered aloud, "it might be worth it just to shut him up."

"*Asiri!*" Kuntur cawed, indignant.

"Puma will not be attempting to attack you, Lord Kuntur. Just as you will not try to swoop down and make off with Dama Katari, correcto?"

At that, Kuntur looked skeptical. Or as skeptical as a large bird of prey could manage.

"But she is so nice and plump," the condor whined.

At his words, Katari uncoiled, rearranging herself into a defensive position.

"*Gracias*," the now agitated snake directed at Kuntur, her eyes thin slits on her narrow face.

Kuntur spread his long wings and clicked his beak at the snake, covering her rock in shadow. In response, Katari hissed menacingly, which caused Puma to scramble up and back away, their large paws kicking up leaves and dust. In their haste, they slammed against the trunk of Kuntur's tree, making the bird lose his balance. The bird staggered and almost toppled off before screeching in terror.

"Puma will *not* eat Kuntur, Kuntur will *not* eat Katari and Katari will *not* bite Puma, oyeron?" Asiri raised her voice in exasperation. "And Asiri can't leave until the ceremony is complete, so can we please get started? The sooner we begin, the sooner you can all leave each other's wretched company."

The animals were suddenly quiet, each staring at her in wide-eyed surprise. She was usually much more patient, but the knowledge that this was the last Communion before her freedom had filled her with anxious anticipation.

"Well," Katari drawled, her voice low and rich. "Anything to get this over with quickly."

When the other two made no complaints, Asiri sighed in relief and moved to a sitting position.

She motioned invitingly to Kuntur, and after a moment, the bird flew down from his perch to settle behind her. He shifted forward, placing his bulky head over her right shoulder, playfully nipping at her hair.

Katari slithered from the stone over the dirt path to wind her way around Asiri's left ankle and calf, which was crossed over her right thigh.

Finally, Puma stalked over to sit at her left side, and Asiri dug her fingers into their remarkably soft coat.

"Gracias amiges," she murmured, letting her eyes flutter shut. She felt Katari squeeze her leg a little tighter, while Kuntur nuzzled against her with his beak. Puma leaned more heavily into her side, feeling even warmer than the already sweltering day.

"Let's see what the universo has to tell us," Asiri said, ready to let the animals transport her to the very center of it.

Her first step was to visit the spirit realm of Uhku Pacha, the underworld. The biggest danger in Uhku Pacha was the supay, demonios that existed solely to torment the souls of the dead.[5]

Asiri did not fear them, as she knew Katari would protect her. That was one reason having all three of her spirit guides was so important to the ritual. Without them, she would wander the

---

5. "Supay" is also the Quechua god of death, and ruler of Ukhu Pacha. He is not viewed as evil, but as a necessary part of existence.

realms alone, lost, and vulnerable. But with them by her side, she was an invited guest, and protected.

The first thing that she did was unearth some soil in front of her with her left hand. As Uhku Pacha held a connection to both death and new life, the realm was intrinsically connected with harvesting. Therefore disruptions on the surface of the world were a link to the one below.

Then, Asiri removed a small leather pouch from her side which had a carved bone stopper. She pulled it out with her teeth, and the stinging scent of alcohol wafted up her nose, burning the insides of her nostrils. She poured a little into the upset earth before her, a tribute and peace offering to the supay. No guest should come empty-handed after all. Then she took a small sip herself, in the spirit of sharing.

Once that was complete, she closed her eyes and settled into the meditation ritual. The meditation was easy; it was one of the great benefits of having a shaman for a father. Since she was a child, she practiced traveling within the cosmos of her own mind, and in turn, connecting to the infinite worlds that overlapped one another like a beautifully braided rope.

She allowed her mind to clear, watched her thoughts float by in the inside of her head like pretty clouds, letting them float over her without focusing on any single one in particular. Her body began to relax, feeling as if her legs were melting into the earth beneath her, then her pelvis and belly, then her torso. She no longer felt Katari tangled around her leg, Puma leaning into her side, or Kuntur's heavy head on her shoulder, for she no longer had legs, or sides, or shoulders. She was nothing and everything, and as her body floated away from her consciousness, her heart began pumping slower and slower.

Finally, Asiri died.

COUGAR/
PUMA

CHAPTER 2

ASIRI

A siri did find it rather inconvenient that in order to hear the messages within the center of the universe she had to die each time, but as it was unavoidable, she had grown quite used to it.

Her soul transported from her body and drifted downwards into the underworld, which was, for all intents and purposes, death.

Ukhu Pacha was different each time that she entered. Sometimes she landed in soil, in the midst of endless fertile fields that stretched as far as her eyes could see. When she found herself there, Katari presented in her regular size, long enough to coil around her leg or drape over her shoulders.

Other times Asiri found herself on scorched earth, her bare feet on smoldering lumps of coal that would have burned her flesh, if she had any flesh in that realm to burn. Sparks of flame and ash fell from the sky, and shadowed visions of the supay lurked in the periphery of her sight. In those times, Katari was an enormous presence by her side, the width of her body larger than a horse, her length so expansive that she could have stretched from one end of Asiri's village to the other.

This time, Asiri found herself in her favorite depiction of Ukhu Pacha, in the middle of a maize field, a large patch of it cleared in the shape of a chakana.[1]

In the center of the Andean cross was a heavy wooden table, absolutely overflowing with ripe and ready crops. She could see clay bowls of tumbling potatoes of varying sizes and colors, from curling, golden-yellow tubers no bigger than her pinky, to fat purple bulbs larger than both her hands combined. There were tall woven baskets overflowing with maize; blanco, amarillo y morado, sometimes the ears boasting kernels of all three colors combined. There were lucuma, aguaymanto, maracuyá y chirimoya fruits, aguaje palms, aji amarillo and purple onions. The table lay scattered with coca leaves too, as well as other herbs and plants.

The air smelled like freshly cut grass, the minty notes of yerba buena, and citrus. There was no sun in the sky—because there was technically not a sky in this realm—but the day was bright and balmy.

Asiri knew that this was the layer of the underworld that Pachamama most resided in, and it was the earth mother's bounty that was displayed so lushly and overtly.[2] Katari was always tiny

---

1. "Chakana" means "bridge," and is often referred to as the "Andean cross." Each arm of the cross represents something different, as does each "step" between the arms. The circle in the center denotes the center of the universe, and the connection or path between all the pachas.

2. Pachamama is the feminine Inca goddess representing the "earth mother" or "mother earth." She presides over fertility, farming, and harvesting, among other things.

in this corner of Ukhu Pacha, like a snakelet, twining around her fingers like a living ring.

First Asiri folded onto her knees, then lightly kissed the ground beneath her feet, quietly thanking Pachamama for her generosity. Rising up, she crossed to the table, which became all the more expansive and impressive the closer she got to it. She looked down the length of the wood longingly, stretching far farther than her eyes could see. After scanning the endless offerings, Asiri selected a single kernel of maize, a purple so deep it appeared black against her dark skin. She brought it to her lips and kissed it as well, then pocketed the talisman for later.

Her time in Ukhu Pacha completed, Asiri began walking through the fields of maize. She was searching for a cave or spring, two things that connected the underworld with the middle world of Kay Pacha. Either would guide her soul back to the earth, where her body sat in meditation.

After a few moments, Katari tugged on her fingers, and motioned in a direction with her head. Asiri changed course, and reached a small mountain, the opening of a cave visible behind hanging vines. She smiled at Katari in gratitude. Asiri was able to speak in the pachas but she found it best not to, as she did not want to attract any added attention from either the supay or the dioses.

Asiri entered the cave and continued to walk. The walls were dark and damp, but carved from stone rather than dirt or mud, which Asiri was grateful for. She had no fear of enclosed spaces, but preferred not to think about the unpredictable nature of a dirt cave when compared to a stone one. As she continued to move, the air became stifling, and a light sweat dampened her temples.

She knew that her earthly form, currently sitting in Kay Pacha, would mirror the perspiration. Finally, the ground beneath her feet slowly began slanting upwards, leading her back to Kay Pacha.

When Asiri emerged, she found herself in front of her meditating body and took a moment to study her motionless form. Like most of her people, her face was a rounded oval shape, with high cheekbones and full lips. Her nose was thin at the top, then tapered to a broad triangle base, the tip curving slightly down. Her eyes pinched in at the inner corners, then bloomed into wide, sideways raindrops. When they were open, they were the color of warm amber. Her gaze drifted over her hair, which was thick and pin straight, usually parted down the center of her head and twisted into two solid braids. Several strands had escaped and floated around her scalp like crackling black lightning. Her skin was a golden bronze, and currently still flushed red over her cheeks from her hike up the mountain. As she had suspected, her forehead was dotted with sweat.

Her spirit form brushed a hand over the top of her body's head, emotion tightening the muscles in her throat. In the waking world, she was often harsh to her body, worried that her flesh was too full or her legs too wide. She found the thickness of her brows and flatness of her face inelegant compared to some of her friends. She lamented the plain black clothing that all members of the Casa de Murmuros wore, and longed for the bright, joyous colors of regular people living their regular, normal lives.

However, in viewing herself outside of her body, she could feel nothing but affection and gratitude. This was the body that housed her, that moved her forward in Kay Pacha. Her legs were strong and muscular and had brought her to the top of the Andes, never faltering in her hike. The arms that drifted to her side were soft and full, and felt nice wrapped around others in an embrace. Her hips were the perfect size for balancing children, who loved being hoisted up and carried with their little hands wrapped around her braids, heads tucked against her breast.

Asiri smiled at the young woman in front of her, then lifted her hand off her head, quietly vowing to be a bit kinder to herself upon waking.

When Puma noticed her presence, their spirit form rose from her side, shaking out their lumbering limbs and crossing to her. Since Asiri still needed to reach Hanan Pacha after this realm, she could not yet re-enter her body, and as a courtesy, Puma joined her on the spirit plane instead. She sunk her fingers into the soft fur at the top of their head, rubbing firmly. They learned their form into hers, and Asiri could feel the rumbling of their satisfied purrs vibrating her entire being, and it made her smile.

"Where shall we travel to today, amige?" she asked them. Puma stretched, their front talons digging into the dirt as their spine curved into a pronounced hook, rump in the air, tail wagging about lazily. As they settled back, their spirit body began lengthening and expanding until they were a little over twice their normal size. Asiri bowed her head in appreciation before settling herself upon their back.

Without warning—or answer—Puma bounded forward into the rainforest.

Trees blurred as they traveled, impossibly fast and impossibly far. Asiri felt the contracting and releasing of Puma's bunching muscles as they propelled them forward. She caught glimpses of alerce and pehuén trees blurring by, as well as the startled glances of spectacled bears, vicuñas y guanacos. Even though Asiri and Puma did not have any physical presence at the moment, Asiri knew that most animals were in tune enough with the various levels of existence to sense their proximity.

When they reached the town of Ollantaytambo, Asiri assumed that Puma would continue traveling southeast towards Vinicunca, as they knew that it was one of her favorite places.[3] They had traveled there before, the verdant scenery of the Andean jungle giving way to rolling stone mountains, as brightly colored as a bouquet of fine flowers. The hills boasted streaks of yellows, reds, teals, pinks, oranges, and greens, like rainbow-colored temples over rocky floors. The last time that Asiri had communed with the sacred three, she had taken a brightly colored pebble from the top of one of the slopes as her talisman of Kay Pacha.

However, Puma changed directions entirely, and began traveling west. They began picking up speed, the scenery no longer visible but for a violent blur, and yet Asiri was not afraid. In fact, she leaned forward, gripping Puma's fur more tightly. She was excited! They had never gone this far before, and she could not wait to see what Puma was leading her toward. After seconds—or an eternity, as time meant nothing in the spirit realm—Asiri felt Puma slow their pace. She noticed that they were passing a considerable expanse of desert, and Asiri became fascinated by the endless, arid sheet of sand that extended as far as the eye could see. But still, they did not stop. They continued, passing small towns, then larger villages.

---

3. A place in Peru often referred to as "Rainbow Mountain."

Then, the air began turning humid, the temperature warm and muggy. They slowed even further and Asiri noticed that they were traveling parallel to a long river, where she could see a bustling, colorful village. Buildings and houses painted in various bright hues rose up across the landscape, and tassels, lanterns and streamers hung from posts that framed the river. She could just barely make out the people, who were also a blur of color and pattern in their eye-catching clothing. Then Asiri's eyes widened as, just past the buildings and people, she saw a sprawling expanse of blue.

"Puma!" she cried out in wonder. "Is that the ocean?"

Asiri felt, rather than heard, Puma's affirming chuckle.

She could not stop staring. She could barely even blink as Puma slowed, their enormous feet leaving behind the whisper of paw prints on the sand below them, vanishing almost as quickly as they appeared. She simply sat, her mouth agape and eyes wide in amazement.

"I have always wanted to see the ocean," she whispered, her voice barely audible over the roaring crash of the waves. As each one hit the shore it left bubbling white foam in its wake, until pulled back into the ocean or absorbed by the sand underneath. It was fascinating, and beautiful.

"I rarely come out this far, it is not the environment for my people," Puma confessed. "The town we passed was the one of Pisqu."[4]

---

4. "Pisqu" is the Quechua word for the Peruvian city of Pisco. "Pisqu" means "little bird" in Quechua.

Asiri noticed that even their spirit form seemed clammy with the muggy heat that surrounded them. She quickly slid off their back and gasped as she registered the springy warmth of the sand under her feet.

"But if this is to be your last spirit travel with me, then I wanted it to be memorable," they continued.

Asiri's mouth dropped open.

"How did you know this was my last Communion?" she asked them, surprised. She hadn't mentioned it to anyone except her father yet.

Puma merely blinked their large golden eyes at her.

Of course, Asiri thought to herself. They are the guardians of Kay Pacha, the animal symbol of wisdom and intelligence. Of course, they knew of her intentions. Asiri found herself deeply moved by their gesture.

"Gracias," she told them, bowing deeply.

As much as Asiri wanted to linger, there was still the final realm to visit, and she could not stay in Kay Pacha forever. So, she made her way to the breaking tide and let the cool water bathe her feet, tickling between her toes.

Asiri bent and found a tiny seashell, the size of her thumbnail, and kissed it before pocketing it next to her kernel of maize. Then, with one last long glance at the ocean, Asiri turned to Puma.

"Are there any arcoiris nearby?" she asked them.

They nodded their large cat head and motioned for her to mount once again, then began carrying her down the beach. Asiri was glad that they could sense a rainbow near them, as both rainbows and lightning were connections from Kay Pacha, the earth, to Hanan Pacha, the heavens above. However, the travel through a rainbow was far more pleasurable than that of lightning, and Asiri was relieved that it was an option that day.

Soon the two were traveling through an area with a light spray of rain, and both Asiri and Puma tilted up their heads to allow their faces to be bathed in its refreshing mist. The sun was bright and between the water and its rays, a beautiful rainbow stretched between the earth and the skies.

Sliding off their back, Asiri thanked Puma once again for their aid, and then began climbing the rainbow arc towards the final pacha.

Hanan Pacha was the least tangible of the three realms. It was made up of the infinite cosmos and home to the sun god Inti and his wife, the moon goddess Mama Killa, among others.[5]

Asiri climbed high enough that all she could see below her was clouds. That was when Kuntur found her. He was soaring through the sky, great black wings spread wide, flapping with so much strength that Asiri knew he could reach the very heavens themselves.

Which was handy, since that was exactly where they were going.

Like Puma, Kuntur had also expanded his form until he was enormous compared to his earthly body. He grew large enough

---

5. Inti is the masculine Inca god of the sun. Known as the patron god of the Inca empire.

Mama Killa is the feminine Inca goddess of the moon. In Quechua, "Mama Killa" means "Mother Moon." She is best known as the Goddess of Women, for she presides over marriage, menstruation, and is the defender/protector of women.

to scoop Asiri up delicately between his claws, then began flying them both higher.

The transition from Kay Pacha to Hanan Pacha was always abrupt. One moment, Asiri could feel cool gusts of wind on her face and skin, pulling insistently at her hair and clothing, hearing the rushing of the air, thunderous to her ears.

And then, silence.

Once she and Kuntur broke through to the upper realm, there was no noise, no wind, no discernible movement. Just a deep, dark stretch of endless, infinite darkness, studded with equally limitless stars, moons, and planets. She could see Inti in the distance and averted her gaze out of respect.

Kuntur moved them deeper into the realm and they passed by beautiful burning orbs and slow-moving meteorites. They turned to see the earth below them, so blue and green and beautiful in the distance.

She and Kuntur floated, weightless, not only in body but in mind. Any problems, any worries, any doubt that existed in Kay Pacha ceased to exist in the upper world. The tension melted from her spirit body, all the remnants of aches and pains and anxiety that she had brought with her from her corporeal one simply melted away. The darkness enveloped her in warmth, comfort, and love. She was made of the same stuff as the divine, and it was, well, divine.

As they floated away from earth, Asiri began to forget that it was her home. It looked just like a pretty-colored gem, so very far away. Slowly she began forgetting other bits and pieces of herself, too. They were inconsequential in this realm. Her purpose began dissolving from her mind. Why was she there? Who was she? It didn't matter, because nothing mattered. She had always been in Hanan Pacha, and would always be in Hanan Pacha. It was a part of her, and she it, and it was where she belonged.

Asiri shut her eyes.

Suddenly, a sharp pain registered on her right bicep. With a small, soundless yelp, Asiri opened her eyes to see Kuntur glaring at her. He had nipped at her with his beak. Asiri looked at her shoulder, where she was sure that she would find a small rivulet of blood, but found only smooth flesh. She had forgotten for a moment that she could not bleed in the realm.

Asiri shot Kuntur a wry grin. Thank the dioses for her spirit guides! This is what they were for, to guard her in the realms that were not her own, and to protect her in the one that was. She inclined her head at Kuntur in gratitude, and he just huffed, shaking his feathers.

Asiri noticed a thin ray of sunlight traveling through the dark, reaching them both. Plucking a piece of the beam, she severed the connection between it and Inti, turning the piece of sunlight into a solid gold sliver in her palm.

She kissed it, thanking the dioses for their blessings, and then removed the other two tokens. She placed the kernel of corn that she collected in Ukhu Pacha within the smooth, inner curve of the seashell from Kay Pacha. Then, with as much force as she could muster, Asiri pierced the two of them with the sliver of gold, combining them as best she could between her fingers.

Asiri was ready to travel to the center of the pachas, the inner realm of the universe.

The center of the universe felt like being back inside the womb.

At least, Asiri assumed that it did. She actually didn't remember being inside the womb. But she imagined it felt something like this.

She was cradled by life, and the earth, existence, and the folds and fabrics of space and time itself. She was in the center of north, south, east, and west, between the layers of Ukhu Pacha, Kay Pacha, and Hannan Pacha. She glided on the air and floated on the sea and was buried in the soil. She was everything, and she was nothing; she was no one, and she was everyone.

It felt like coming home.

The center of all things was always quiet and tranquil, but if Asiri listened hard enough, she could sometimes hear the whispered warnings of the universe. She existed calmly in nothingness, waiting patiently.

When the warning began, it was quiet, like the sound of an ant's footsteps over a blade of grass. It was delicate, a barely there whisper tickling the inside of her brain. Then it grew louder, but only slightly, like breadcrumbs falling on a wooden floor. A sound that would have been imperceptible had she not been in such stillness. Then it grew louder still, like the vibrations of a yawn, then the faint cracking of knuckles. She felt everything tremble around her, and inside her, and the sound grew to be the rattling of a kite in a strong wind, then a horse's running hoof beats.

The vibration became stronger.

Rolling wheels of carts over cobblestones, jostling her without movement. Then it was the crashing of ocean waves, a feeling she had only recently experienced. Asiri shook. The feeling of tumbling stones over the sides of mountains, mudslides and toppling trees. Asiri began trembling, not with fear, for she knew she was safe where she was, but by a larger force, a force of nature.

Then, with an earth-shattering crack, the rumbling stopped, and Asiri opened her eyes in the waking world, heart racing in her chest and beads of sweat dripping down her face.

CONDOR/
CÓNDOR

Chapter 3

Asiri

"There's going to be an earthquake," she told her father, the shaman, when she returned to the Casa de Murmuros.[1] "A big one," she warned, grabbing a ripe melocotón and taking a big, juice-filled bite. She had packed many provisions for her hike into the Andes, long strips of dried meat and queso fresco that she was forced to finish the first day, so it wouldn't go bad in the heat. She had taken lucuma and tostadas, hard-boiled eggs, and dried kernels of corn. But both the physical trip and meditative journey always left her feeling ravenous for a few days after a Communion with the sacred three.

"Cuando?" her father asked her, his wiry dark brows drawn low.

"I don't know when," she answered honestly, wiping some sticky juice off of her chin with the back of her right hand. "But if it was a warning, we should have enough time to alert all the

---

1. Inca shamans are seen as a type of "holy men," spiritual advisors, and healers, often using natural medicines for their practices and rituals.

villages, urge them to stockpile provisions, and reinforce weak homes or buildings."

"Si, si, of course," her father said, waving his hand in front of his face dismissively.

Asiri frowned. "You *will* tell the other villages, won't you?" she asked him uncertainly. The mountainous area in which they lived boasted dozens of small villages and towns, and while the entire realm was susceptible to quakes, those who lived on the elevated peaks held the greatest risk should disaster strike. But if they received warning, those villages would tell the next, and the next, spreading as far as the northern peaks and the western coasts. The sooner the warning went out, the more likely it was that everyone could prepare in time.

"Claro," he replied, smoothly. "They will know. But there are a few who would pay good money to learn of something like this first and get a head-start on gathering supplies that they need."

"If you do that, they will have a chance to hoard materials and provisions from the others!" Asiri cried out, horrified. "It's not fair!"

"This is what we do," her father reminded her coldly. "It is our job, and we get paid for doing it well."

Asiri knew that her father was an opportunistic man, more concerned with money and status than community and even family. She couldn't be sure if he had always been this way, or if the death of her mother when she was young had turned him into the man before her. All she knew was that most shamanes cared little for status or wealth, like her father did.

He had made being a holy man into a business.

When she was young, she had not minded using her gift to help him. She thought it was a way that they could grow closer. And for a while, it worked. When she did well, he paid attention to her. He would dine with her, ask her questions about her journeys and discoveries. But it soon became apparent that he was only interested in what she could do for him, and not in who she was as a person. She didn't think her father was a wicked man, just not a particularly good one either. And she didn't want to spend another moment in Casa de Murmuros, working under his thumb.

"It's *your* job," she told him. "Not mine, not anymore. That was my last commission, remember?"

Her father made a dismissive noise, sucking his teeth. "I thought you would get over that," he told her derisively. "I thought if you did a big job, commune with the holy three, that you would remember your gift."

"I have never forgotten my gift," she told him honestly. "I just don't like the way it's being used here, or the way you are using it. I want to be free to make my own choices."

Asiri made herself look him in the eye, even though, internally, she trembled.

"No," her father said.

"No?" Asiri repeated, confused.

"No, you cannot leave Casa de Murmuros. I won't allow it," her father replied, turning his back on her, moving towards the exit.

"It is my life, and my decision, you can't just—" Asiri started, but he whirled around, his eyes angry and cold.

"*I will not allow it,*" he spat out, aggressively stepping towards her, making Asiri shrink back. When she looked up to meet his gaze, he loomed over her menacingly and appeared taller than before. His eyes drew into thin slits, a flash of violent light sparking within their depths. There was a deep groove carved in between his brows, fissures cracking the skin around his eyes and tight mouth, betraying both his ire and his age.

His considerable appearance shocked Asiri. She had seen him angry and disappointed with some of the other members of the Casa before. Having never felt his ire with such force, Asiri finally understood why the other members of the Casa feared her father.

But Asiri was not a little girl anymore. She was a twenty-seven-year-old woman.

Steeling her shoulders back, she made herself look her father in the eye.

"You promised," she ground out through her teeth. "When I first mentioned this to you, you said that you would give me the percentage of earnings that are rightfully mine."

Since she was a child, any job she worked in the Casa had earned her ten percent of the commission fee. Her father told her he was saving the money for her in a personal trust, and she never had cause to ask for access to the funds before. But the quick calculations that she made in her head had come up with an impressive number, enough to get her started anywhere she chose.

Her father scoffed. "What would you need that moneda for?" he asked her. "You have everything you need here in the Casa."

Asiri's heart sank.

"No, no, I think it's best I hold on to it for you," Kallpa Yupanqui continued.

Asiri's hands went numb at the realization that he never intended to relinquish her money to her. And a small, treacherous little voice in the back of her head wondered if he even set aside a portion of the earnings for her at all. In that moment, it would not have surprised Asiri to learn that he never had any intention of allowing her access to the money. The thought disintegrated any fight left in her.

"You will stay here, where you belong," he said absently, the matter clearly already settled in his mind.

"Pero—" she tried one more time.

"Do you understand me?" he barked at her, his words trembling with force.

Taken aback, Asiri simply nodded. "Si papá," she answered softly.

She watched as his shoulders relaxed. Then he reached out and patted a hand over her arm before turning and leaving.

Asiri stood there for a long while, still shocked that her father would deny her the simple luxury of freedom. Guilt crept across her skin like the tendrils of vines, pricking her with sharp thorns.

I should have argued more, she thought. *I should have convinced him. Why didn't I try harder?*

But Asiri knew it would have been useless. There was no arguing with her father. Numbly, she left the kitchen, where her Kallpa had found her, and moved through the expanse of the temple to her room. When she crossed inside it, she quietly closed her door and braced her back against the hard wood. After a moment, she allowed her legs to fold, sliding down until she sat on the cool stone ground. Looping her arms around her shins, she dropped her head onto her knees.

She didn't cry. She was too numb to cry.

Of course, he never planned to let her leave. She was far too valuable to Casa de Murmuros and he would never allow her to stop. It wasn't like she had a plan for leaving anyway, apart from "being her own person and living her own life."

Really, it wasn't so bad, living in the Casa's compound, tucked away in the Andes. The mountains were beautiful, full of all sorts of animals and birds that she could speak to and learn from. Their meals were always delicious: rice, quinoa, potatoes, and maize grown right in their very garden, with spices, peppers and aji amarillo. Others brought produce and game seasonally to them, often as tribute from those seeking to curry favor with her father. The days were warm and comforting. Inti blessed them with enveloping sunlight. The nights were often cool and refreshing, with nothing but the sounds of the forest to lull her to sleep. It wasn't an awful life.

Except for the fact that she didn't have many friends; human ones, that is. Asiri had been born and raised in La Casa, and trained in Creature Communing since she was a child. Interaction with the outside world was rare, and she often kept to those who worked in the Casa, either as one of their members, boasting their own special gifts, or those who supported and maintained the compound, like the cooks and cleaners. The majority of her youth was spent training under her father and her tutors, and by the time she was old enough to join the other members, they had already made friend groups amongst themselves, and were hesitant to let in the daughter of their boss. They were never unkind to her, just distant. Not to mention that she found herself increasingly wary of her father's approach to what the Casa did. She had always been eager to help others, but the direction Casa de Murmuros had been taking as of late felt a bit more self-serving than selfless.

I could leave anyway, she thought to herself.

It was a startling, almost laughable idea.

So what if I don't have my funds? she thought. Sure, the money would have made her transition into "ordinary life" much simpler, but she was smart and capable. She could make her own way, couldn't she?

Maybe. It was a frightening proposition, going out into the "real world" alone, inexperienced, and penniless. And yet, she wouldn't starve, her animal friends would not allow it. And she could sleep outside in the elements better than most people could. She knew animals would happily and willingly share their warm dens. Most predators wouldn't attack her, not when she could speak to them and bargain for her life. She could find her way to a town, a village, a city, somewhere, and start anew. She was young and strong, she could find work, and earn her own money, no need for the funds that her father may or may not have saved for her.

But where could I go? she wondered. The neighboring towns and villages were out of the question. They were far too close to the Casa, to her father, to make them a viable option. When he realized that she'd left, Kallpa Yupanqui would come looking for her. She knew it. And she was too well known around these parts to hide effectively. *The Andes,* she realized, *are out of the question.*

She could travel east, to her favorite rainbow-colored mountains of Vinicunca. It was far enough that most people were unlikely to know who she was, and the towns were large enough that she could blend in with the travelers that frequented the area daily.

But was it far enough? If her father sent someone after her, would she be able to remain hidden well enough to avoid detection?

Asiri shifted on the ground and yelped when something poked her in the fleshy part of her butt. Frowning, she dug into her side pocket, her fingers wrapping around something hard and sharp. When she pulled it out, her mouth dropped open.

It was a seashell. To be more specific, it was the exact, tiny seashell that she had used in her Communion days prior.

Asiri was amazed. Never in her experience with Communing with the sacred three had a tribute ever returned with her to Kay Pacha. They always combined, and then disappeared together. Asiri always assumed that they were the price she needed to pay to reach the center of the universe. But here it was, as real as it was when she had first plucked it from the shores of the coast.

Rubbing the seashell between her fingers, Asiri remembered the village that she had seen when Puma had taken her to the ocean. The one that had built itself on the banks of the long river, leading to the sea. In her mind she saw the brightly colored buildings, the hanging lanterns and woven tapestries, the bustling storefronts, and the intricately embroidered clothing of the people there. She imagined what it would be like to wrap herself in one of the bright, colorful scarves she had seen the women wear.

Quickly, she sat up, holding the shell in front of her like an offering to the dioses.

The coast was so distant from the mountains, and the Casa, that her father would never think of looking for her there! For all he knew, Asiri never had cause to visit that far. And if it weren't for Puma and his final trip, Kallpa would be correct in his assumption. But she now knew the might of the ocean, and the salty taste of the air, and the springy warmth of the sand beneath her feet. She knew that there were ordinary people there, working ordinary jobs and living regular, everyday lives. The kind of life that Asiri envied so very much.

Springing up from the floor, Asiri pocketed the shell once again, deep in her trousers. The path was clear. She was going to go west, to live by the sea. The details about what she would do once she got there could be sorted out later.

Almost without thinking, Asiri took out a large rucksack and began packing her belongings into it. She didn't bother with any of the dark, shapeless robes of the Casa, and grabbed only the travel garments that she was allowed to wear when hiking or Creature Communing. They were still black, but much more comfortable than the robes. Asiri decided that she would get herself some pretty, brightly colored clothing as soon as she was able. A small rebellious thrill rushed through her at the thought, followed by a quick pang of guilt, which she quickly suppressed. There was nothing for her to feel guilty about. When she was out in the real world, with regular people, she would be free to wear whatever she wanted.

After packing her clothes, there were only a few items that Asiri thought about bringing with her. There was a charming teal and gold painting of various animals that a past client had gifted the Casa as thanks for their aid in a theft. She had discovered the culprit thanks to some jacamars in the area; a particularly chismoso breed of birds. The customers paid their fee upon the retrieval of the stolen pottery, but they gifted the painting out of gratitude. Since the artist was practically unknown, and the painting was not very expensive, her father allowed her to keep it in her room.

After placing it carefully in between some of her shirts, she reached under her bed to pull out a long folding pouch. When she first learned that she could speak to animals, it pained her that she could not do much when any of her new friends became ill or injured. Over the years, she had come to assemble a small amount of medicinal items, a needle and thread to sew up injuries, plants and herbs to help numb pain and combat infection. It wasn't much, and Asiri could only help with the mildest of injuries or illnesses, but she did her best whenever she could.

Finally, she opened the delicately carved box that sat on her nightstand and pulled out a simple gold chain that had belonged to her mother. She never wore it in the Casa, or on her jobs, as she was too afraid that she would lose it. It was the only thing she had of her mother's, and she treasured it dearly. However, if she was going to have a fresh start outside of the Casa walls, maybe it would be a nice symbol of her new life.

Asiri peeked out into the hallway to make sure her father's door was closed. Satisfied, she snuck her way to the kitchen and filled another, smaller bag full of food and supplies. Finally, she took a quick look around the room and the home she had grown up in.

Then she turned around, and with every last scrap of her courage, headed towards the coast.

SPECTACLED BEAR/
UKUKU

Chapter 4

Asiri

A siri's father always waited at least three days after her return from communing with the sacred three to schedule another assignment, so she knew she had that much time to escape. She realized that this was because he feared her fatigue would lead to mistakes, rather than because he had an actual interest in her wellbeing, but even so, she had some time. Still, she felt guilty and nervous sneaking out of the Casa de Murmuros, jumping at every crunch of leaves beneath her feet or the rustling of foliage in the wind.

When she was sure that no guards were going to come running to snatch her back to the Casa, she relaxed and took in her surroundings. The surrounding mountains were always alive with conversation, blue and yellow macaws gossiping above the canopy, foxes murmuring amongst themselves about a nest of eggs they could steal if only they could distract the mother long enough. Two llamas chatted as they chewed, one claiming that the grass near the mountain edge was tastier, the other insisting that the low shrub he was munching from was the more flavorful choice. A family of titi monkeys in a cluster of trees were arguing over whose turn it was to look after the infants, while slightly older younglings rolled and tousled along the branches.

Asiri grew up with those sounds. Every morning she awoke to the conversation of birds outside of her window. They unintentionally kept Asiri well-informed on where to find the fattest grubs, which nests blew down by the winds, and whose chicks were ready to fly. The mice inside Casa de Murmuros would excitedly tell her what type of pan the cooks baked for the day, which fruits they served for breakfast. The rats warned her when the dining room was too full, and when she could make her quiet approach without drawing too much attention.

The cats never spoke to her, except to demand more food, or chin scratches. They came to her if they needed something removed from their paws, or had grievances with certain humans. She didn't mind, she rather enjoyed their surly superiority.

Years of practice allowed Asiri to tune out the incessant noise if she so chose. She could push most of the chatter to the back of her mind as a sort of fuzzy background noise. It was soothing most of the time, but she could not shut out if an animal was talking to her directly. That would be like ignoring a human trying to get your attention, nearly impossible, not to mention terribly rude.

But walking in the Andes, most of the animals left her alone. As soon as they realized she was not a danger, they simply disregarded her presence. She heard an occasional "human," or "girl," but said with passing curiosity rather than real interest or fear.

The sun was just starting to set across the mountains when one voice cut through the rest.

"Oh, goodness me. Oh, miercoles," it mumbled.[1]

Asiri paused at the distressed tone and then moved towards the muffled grumbles. She had just broken through a dense cluster of trees when she heard it again.

"Oof, oh Qori. Now you've done it."

In an open patch of grass and bushes, Asiri spotted an ukuku. Her shoulders dropped, the tense muscles unknotting. Ukukus were smaller sized bears, usually not much larger than a human. They had black and brown fur save for lighter colored rings on their face, especially over their eyes, causing some people to refer to them as "spectacled bears." They were kind, shy, and very proper beings, and Asiri had always enjoyed their company.

"Hola, tio," Asiri called out to him respectfully.[2]

The bear jolted and twisted in her direction; his face pinched in surprise. As he turned, Asiri felt her brows furrow together with concern.

"Oh no, my friend, what happened?"

Asiri dropped her bags and approached the bear gingerly. Ukukus were not usually aggressive, but she didn't want to startle him. The poor bear's paw was stuck deep inside an aguaymanto

---

1. "Miercoles" means "Wednesday." However, in this context, it is a way for someone to swear without actually swearing. The beginning of "miercoles," "mier," could easily be finished with "da," to create "mierda," which means "shit." It is like saying "fudge" instead of "fuck."

2. "Tio" means uncle but can be used as a title of respect towards a male elder.

plant. Somehow, he had managed to wrap his limb up in the branches and vines.

"Oh dear. I am so embarrassed," the ukuku said, slowly blinking his sweet brown eyes at her. "You see, I had finished grabbing all the berries from the outside of the bush."

Judging by the amount of discarded shells around the plant in question, Asiri could tell that there had been quite a lot of berries.

"But," continued the bear, not meeting her eyes, "there were still several towards the center of the bush, you see." "And, well, my snout couldn't reach that far, but I thought if I could swipe at them they would roll out..." his voice trailed off.

"I see," Asiri said as somberly as she could, fighting back the smile that was tugging at her lips. She didn't want to embarrass the poor thing any more than he already was. She inched closer. "Perhaps you would permit me to help?"

The ukuku looked up at her. "Oh, if you wouldn't mind. I hate to be a bother, but—"

"Nonsense," Asiri interrupted. "I'd be happy to help."

Asiri kneeled beside the ukuku and reached her hand in next to his, feeling for where the plant wrapped around his paw. She hoped that she could wiggle him free without having to break out her knife. As much as animals trusted her, they were still understandably skittish around anyone with a weapon. Luckily for the both of them, she could feel where the main tangle was located, and after a few moments of twisting and pulling, the ukuku was finally free. He jerked back, landing on his rump with a soft "*umph!*"

"There we are!" Asiri grinned triumphantly. The ukuku blinked at her again, his eyes decidedly more animated.

"Oh, gracias señorita!" he exclaimed. "I would never know peace again if my cousins had to come and find me. I would never have heard the end of it!"

"It was my pleasure," Asiri told him, happy to have helped. "Now, my arms are quite a bit thinner than yours," she remarked, sticking hers back into the large cluster of aguaymanto bushes. "I'm sure I can grab a few more berries!"

Together, she and the ukuku—Qori, he told her—picked several more of the golden berries, dutifully peeling off the leafy shells to find the bittersweet fruit inside. By the time they ate their fill, (Qori a bit more than Asiri) the sun was well down the mountain and darkness began settling over them, stars beginning to stretch and blink in the night sky.

"Do you have a burrow for the night?" Qori asked Asiri, who shook her head.

"I don't mind sleeping under the trees," she answered him honestly, but Qori made a dismissive snuffing sound through his nose.

"You may share with me tonight," he told her, his backside swaying to and fro as he began heading away from the clearing. "The nights grow cold."

Grateful, Asiri followed him until they stopped at a large, towering tree whose roots jutted out proudly from the ground. Roots so big, in fact, that at the base of the tree two overlapped to form an almost cave-like space. Qori crawled in first, turning a few times before settling himself down, then pawed at the ground in front of him for Asiri to join him. She did, snuggling her back against his soft fur. He draped a heavy arm over her, and she felt instantly bathed in warmth. With a happy smile, Asiri fell asleep.

The next morning Qori led Asiri to a happy, bubbling spring where she could fill her waterskin. She felt tempted to wash up a bit as well, but Qori advised her not to.

"I will tell you where my cousins live," he told her. "They have homes all throughout this region, and you will always have a place to stay as you descend. My scent on you will earn you their trust."

Asiri grinned and placed a quick kiss on the top of his furry, spectacled head. "Gracias, amigo," she thanked him, and laughed when he nuzzled her side so hard she almost toppled over. She regained her balance, and with a few more directions from Qori, continued down the mountain.

For the next two days, Asiri made her way through the Andes and headed west. As promised, she found two of Qori's cousins who offered her shelter each night; though it would be more accurate to say that they found her. Qori was right. His scent led them right to her. After three nights of sleeping on the forest floors with the ukukus, she was sure that any creature would be able to smell her a mile away.

"This is as far as we can offer you aid," Qori's cousin Leticia said after the third night of staying with the ukukus. "We are close enough to the base of the mountains that you will not find any other bears to room with; we do not like descending too close to other humans, and the town of Ollantaytambo is not too far away now."

Asiri patted the bear on the head and thanked her again for her hospitality. Leticia butted her smooth head against Asiri's middle.

"Buena suerte, little cub," she said, as Asiri continued down the mountain.

The closer that Asiri came to Ollantaytambo, the louder things became. She had gotten used to the quiet murmurings of the forest, and the hustle and bustle of people was a shock to her system. Despite the change, Asiri wanted desperately to stop in the village to have a proper bath and to sleep on an actual bed, but ultimately decided against it. It was possible that the Casa de Murmuros had noticed her absence by now, and they might have sent a messenger, scout, or guard to track her down. Ollantaytambo would be the first place that they would look.

Instead, Asiri asked a hawk for directions west, and the bird led her to what she claimed would be a reasonable path for a human to take.

The rest of the journey to the coast went surprisingly smoothly. Asiri relied on the sun and the stars to track her progress west and then began asking other migrating birds to direct her towards the ocean. Once she shared some of her rations with them, they were always happy to oblige.

In the first week of travel, Asiri was close enough to towns and villages that she came across other people traveling in merchant carts pulled by guanacos. Once she proved that she was quite skilled at cleaning the dirt and debris caught on the footpads of the animals and trimming their nails without complaint, many invited her to ride along with them.

In the second week, she slept in barns and stables with cows, goats, and sheep that offered her lodging in exchange for food, picking burrs out of coats, and other small favors.

Towards the end of her third week of travel, Asiri came across a rather large lake. Dropping all her belongings, she placed her hands on her hips and scowled at it. The last bird had been quite clear. If she wanted to reach the coast, this was the path she needed to take. However, her helpful winged friend hadn't mentioned an enormous lake, having seemed to have forgotten that Asiri could not fly.

Asiri looked left, then right, and her scowl deepened. She couldn't swim across the lake, not with all of her belongings, but walking around its expanse would add days to her journey.

She sighed. There was nothing else to do. Bending to pick her packs back up, she startled when a scratchy voice called out from near the water.

"Oh, *please*," she heard it say. "I promise not to eat you, all right? I just need your help!"

"You want me to willingly jump into your open mouth?" Asiri heard an incredulous voice reply. "I wasn't hatched yesterday!"

Scanning the lake shore, Asiri spotted the voices. The first was an adult caiman, her small body halfway out of the water. The other voice was from a small, brown and white finch perched on a nearby tree.

"Por favor!" the caiman called out a bit desperately. "I can't stand it anymore, and I can't reach it myself!"

"Absolutely not," the finch replied with a scoff, before flying away.

"No! Wait!" the caiman called, then collapsed onto the ground with a groan.

"Hola," Asiri said softly, approaching the creature. She was about six feet long with a tan body and dark brown markings. Her eyes were a muddled green.

"Oh!" the caiman startled. "Hola," she replied.

"Is everything all right? I couldn't help but overhear ..." Asiri let her voice trail off into a question.

The caiman released a heavy sigh through her nose.

"Well, you see, I had a fish a few days ago," she explained. "And a rather large fish bone got stuck between my teeth."

The caiman opened her jaws wide, and Asiri peered into her mouth.

"It hurts terribly," the caiman continued. "And I can't even eat. It hurts so much! I was trying to convince that bird to hop in my mouth and pluck it out, but he wouldn't."

The poor thing sounded so defeated, and Asiri thought that if caimans could cry, this one's eyes would be filled with tears.

"If you like, I would be happy to try to help you," Asiri told her. All at once, the caiman brightened.

"Oh, would you? I would appreciate it so much!"

"Of course," Asiri said, rummaging through her rucksack for her healing kit. Once she located it, she drew out a long pair of tweezers. Then, she sat cross-legged so that the caiman could rest her head on her lap. The large reptile opened her mouth again.

"Iss to-ars da bak," the caiman tried to say, mouth still agape.

Asiri noticed the offending fish bone right away. It had indeed gotten stuck between two of the caiman's teeth, but also managed to wedge itself into her gum as well. Asiri winced in sympathy.

"I see it," she said evenly. "Now, this might hurt, but you cannot close your mouth while my hands are inside it, all right?"

The caiman nodded slightly. "Promith," she murmured.

As quickly and deftly as she could, Asiri reached in and plucked the object from between her teeth, having to wiggle it a bit to dislodge it. The caiman grumbled, but as promised, did not move to shut her jaw. With a forceful yank, the bone finally gave way.

"There we are!" Asiri said triumphantly.

The caiman blinked up at Asiri several times, before slowly shutting her mouth. Asiri watched as she moved it back and forth, then clenched and unclenched her jaw. Finally, she regarded Asiri with a toothy grin.

"You did it! You really did it! Oh, thank you so much, amiga!" she cried.

Asiri smiled right back at her. "You are very welcome," she replied.

"Is there anything I can do to repay you? Anything at all?" the caiman asked.

Asiri shook her head. "No payment necessary," she assured her, happy to be of assistance.

"Oh, please, there must be something that I can do," she insisted.

"Not unless you know of a way that I can cross this lake with all of my things," she admitted.

The caiman's eyes twinkled. "You wait right here!" she said, diving back into the water.

Asiri shrugged, but did as was told, content to sit under the warm sun. A few moments later, the caiman returned, bringing with her two friends and a floating plank of wood.

"Look!" she called out, lumbering back out of the water. "You can place your belongings on that, and we will push it across. And you can hold on to me, and I will cross the lake with you!"

Asiri felt incredibly impressed, and very grateful. "That is wonderful!" she cried out. "It will save me so much time!"

Quickly, Asiri took off her shoes and tunic, stuffing them in one of her packs. Then, she placed all of her belongings on the wood, thanking the additional two caimanes for their assistance. Finally, she waded into the water, gasping a little at the coolness against her warm skin. Then she slung her right arm over her new friend.

"Ready?" the caiman grinned.

"Ready," Asiri confirmed.

As soon as they began moving, however, Asiri realized that she had in fact *not* been ready. She let out a little squeal as they began propelling through the water at a speed much faster than she had expected. The water from the lake bathed her face in a fine spray, and Asiri couldn't help but laugh.

"Where are you heading, amiga?" the caiman asked as they crossed.

"Home," Asiri answered, her heart as full as the lake itself. "I'm going home."

HUMMINGBIRD/ COLIBRÍ

CHAPTER 5

ASIRI

O n her twenty-sixth day of traveling, Asiri found the river
she was looking for.

She knew it was the river that she had seen with Puma, even
though, if she was being honest with herself, it didn't look all
that different from all the other rivers that she had passed in her
journey. But somehow, she knew that *this* was the river that was
going to lead her to that darling little town off the coast.

To her new home.

Asiri dropped all her belongings and made her way to the water.
Cupping the gurgling stream in her hands, she brought it to her
lips and drank deeply, then repeated the action until she'd sated
her thirst. Finally, she scrubbed at her face and splashed her arms
with the cool water, trying to remove as much travel dust and
grime as she possibly could.

As she sat back from the water, she noticed an alarming amount
of ropes which looped from one tree to another, all intersecting
and crossing above each other over the river. She craned her neck
and saw that the strange rope contraptions fastened from as far
back to as far forward of the river as she could see and seemed to
serve no particular purpose. They certainly didn't look decorative,

but Asiri couldn't think of what possible purpose they could serve.

With a shrug, Asiri turned her mind to whether or not it would be possible to wash her long black hair, when she suddenly heard a tiny yelp.

"Help me!" a small voice cried out in panic.

Asiri sprang up and swiveled in place, trying to find the voice.

"Help, help!" she heard again, but it seemed to be coming from the river itself.

He was so small that she almost missed him, a tiny, flapping blur of color floating down with the current. Asiri immediately jumped into the river, the water at first reaching mid-calf, then coming all the way up to her waist. The cold overwhelmed her muscles, and she sucked a sharp breath in through her teeth, moving against the force as best she could. Her heart thundered in her ears, and her belly cramped with worry that she would not reach the struggling creature before he floated further down the stream. When she was almost to where the current was dragging him, Asiri reached; her shoulder screaming as she stretched as far as she possibly could, praying that it would be enough to grasp him in time. Then, a small body bumped into her open palm, and she closed her fingers gently, lifting him up and above the water before slowly making her way back to dry land.

He was a tiny thing, even as far as hummingbirds go. His feathers, soaked and plastered against his frail frame were a mixture of emerald, orange, and violet plumage. His body seemed to vibrate, but Asiri couldn't tell if it was the feel of his thunderous little heartbeat underneath her fingers, or if he was shivering from the cold river water. She cupped her hands around him, trying to loan the creature some of her heat.

"Are you all right?" a masculine voice called out, and Asiri lifted her gaze from the hummingbird, expecting to see another forest creature who had witnessed her icy plunge. Instead, to her great surprise, the voice had come from a man.

A very, very attractive man.

He stood well over six feet, with wavy black hair that covered the top of his forehead and ears. His skin was a deep bronze, his chin and jaw dusted with the barest hint of a shadow. The belted, short sleeve tunic he wore hit just below his knee, giving Asiri a glimpse of broad shoulders, muscled arms, and toned, strong calves.

Instinctively, she looked down at herself. The old, dusty travel clothes that she had been wearing for the last few weeks were clinging to her soaking wet body, dripping in murky brown rivulets to the ground. She didn't remember dunking her head underwater, but she must have slipped in her panic to get to the hummingbird in time because her hair lay plastered against her cheeks, neck, and shoulders. Heat burned in her face as she imagined the picture she must be painting, resembling a dirty wet fish rather than a normal human girl.

But you're not exactly normal anyway, are you? she asked herself.

As surreptitiously as she could, Asiri used her left hand to shove her hair away from her face, being careful not to jostle the little body in her right palm any more than she needed to.

"Are you all right?" The man repeated, his voice raspy and sweet, reminding her of burnt honey. Goose pimples erupted all over her skin at the sound.

What is wrong with me?

"I—"" she started, holding out the little hummingbird in front of her, as if that was an answer to all his questions. In a few short steps, the man was standing a breath away from her, cupping his palms around her open hand. Asiri suppressed a shiver at his warm flesh against her cold, clammy skin.

"You saved her," he said, softly, almost reverently, smoothing a finger along the hummingbird's form. It continued to lie panting softly in her hand. "She looks stunned. That must have taken a lot out of her." He examined the bird with quick, practiced movements which made Asiri's eyebrows raise. "I think she'll be all right, though," he finished with a soft smile.

"He," she corrected instinctively, then winced. There was no reason why she should know that the creature in her hand was male, but the man only laughed.

"He, then," the man replied. "Did you know that hummingbirds' hearts beat over 50 times per second?"

Asiri's mouth dropped open. No, she didn't know that.

"Every second?" she asked, and the man nodded, looking pleased.

He lifted his eyes to hers and smiled. "How about you?" he asked. "Are you feeling well?"

At this distance, Asiri could see the thick cluster of his lashes that shadowed his impossibly dark brown eyes. He had a soft beauty mark just below his bottom lip. His very full bottom lip. She swallowed hard, knowing she was blinking at him like a fool, but could not for the life of her get herself to respond.

His brows furrowed, cutting a deep crease in the center of his forehead. "I'm Dario," he said gently. "What's your name?"

"Asi—"" she began to answer, when a gravelly, cantankerous voice interrupted her.

"Oh, sure, chat up the girl, why don't you! Nobody cares if old Marco is dying here!"

"Que?" Asiri startled, jumping back from Dario, but it wasn't he who had spoken.

"Asike?" he repeated, misunderstanding her.

"No, no, I—"" she began again.

"I should be with my family! I have over 400 children, you know. They'll be wondering where I am, animal abductor!"

Asiri had been so distracted admiring Dario that she hadn't noticed he was wearing a sling across his chest. From the folded fabric, a fuzzy but grumpy head poked out, baring its teeth.

"I won't stand for this, you know! It is one thing to kidnap me from my home, it is another to make me witness pathetic attempts at human mating rituals! Cease your flirtations and put me down!"

"We're not," Asiri began to argue, frowning at the animal, which she could now identify as a cuy.[1]

Dario scratched the back of his head with his hand. "Uh, we're not what?" he asked her.

Asiri had not prepared herself for this aspect of her new life. She had decided with utter certainty that she did not want anyone in her new town to know of her abilities. If no one knew that she had the talent of speaking to animals, then no one could abuse

---

1. A "cuy" is a guinea pig. In Peru, while cuy can be pets, they are most often raised to be eaten. However, this particular guinea pig is in no danger of becoming a meal.

her gift. But Asiri had thought that she would have more time to prepare herself before reaching the village and her new home. Larger towns and villages had fewer animals than the forest, so she naturally assumed she could avoid the majority of them for a while, until she had settled in. She didn't expect the first person she would run into would be holding an old, angry guinea pig!

So, before she could explain that she wasn't talking to Dario, she snapped her jaw shut and gave a quick shake of her head.

"Nada," she told him quickly. "Sorry."

"You will be sorry, pitiful human, if you don't have this loath-some creature release me at once!"

"What is this?" she asked Dario, motioning to the guinea pig.

"This is Pepe," Dario responded, reaching around to cup the animal's little body through the sling. The cuy shrieked.

"My name is Marco! Marco Ignacio Lorenzo Gonzales Palacios de la Cruz! Not *Pepe*! How dare you!"

Asiri's left eye began to twitch as she did her best to ignore the ornery guinea pig. Here she was, so close to her destination, in front of an absolutely gorgeous man, moments away from the start of her new life, and she was already messing everything up. She wasn't going to let her gift, or an ill-natured guinea pig, ruin this for her.

"My name is Asiri," she said in a rush. "I'm trying to get to the town of Pisqu."

Asiri didn't think that Dario could get any more handsome, but when his face erupted into a wide grin, she realized she had been wrong. His smile was like the first sip of chocolate caliente, warm and sweet with just a hint of spice. Butterflies tumbled hard in her belly, and she licked her lips nervously.

As he opened his mouth to say something...
So did the damn cuy.

GUINEA PIG/
CUY

CHAPTER 6

DARIO

Dario woke up that morning the way he did most mornings, happy and hopeful despite the multitude of chores that he needed to accomplish throughout the day. He had expected to visit his clinic, take care of his patients, then rope his sister Tamya into watching them for a few hours while he foraged for much needed medicinal herbs and plants in the forest.

What he had not expected that day was to run into the most beautiful woman that he had ever seen in his life.

When he first saw her, moving through the river water, he had thought that she must surely be a sirena; a vision, plucked straight out of his most perfect fantasy. Her skin was a golden bronze, her hair as dark as the night sky, falling determinedly to her waist. Her eyes were wide and tilted at the edges, her lips lush and full. When she had pulled herself from the rushing current, her plain clothing clung to her form, outlining small, high breasts and thick, rounded thighs. Surely, she was not a real, flesh and blood woman. The second that he approached her, she would show her true form and drag him to his watery death.

For a moment, Dario thought it might be worth it, to be wrapped up in those limbs for even the slightest moment.

But then she shivered, lifting her hands to her face to peer at something. At that moment, Dario realized that she *was* real and had jumped into the river to save something. To save an *animal*. That small action made her even better in his eyes than any fantasy that he could have concocted. So, he approached her only to find she was even more lovely up close.

He was as gentle as possible, but she seemed stunned and distracted. Even so, he tried his best to get her to speak to him, wanting both to make sure that she was all right, and to get to know her a little better.

"My name is Asiri," she finally told him. "I'm trying to get to the town of Pisqu."

An overwhelming sense of relief flooded Dario's being. The river goddess was going to his town! He would see her again!

"That is where I live!" he told her, doing his best (and failing) to keep the excitement from his voice. "You're not far now."

She blinked long lashes at him, droplets of water slipping from them and splashing delicately onto her cheeks. His head swam, and he scrambled to think of something else, anything else, to say to her.

"I am the town's animal healer," he finally blurted. If his skin were any lighter, he was sure she would see the rising flush on his cheeks. "That is why I have Pepe here," motioning to the injured cuy in his sling, hoping she didn't find him too odd.

"Oh," was all she replied, until Pepe squealed again, causing her to flinch.

Is she afraid of animals? Dario wondered. That couldn't be right. She had gone out of her way to save the colibrí. Maybe just rodents, then? He knew most people didn't find them as sweet and cute as he did, but disappointment still lay in his heart like a stone. *Oh well, I suppose no one is perfect,* he thought. *Dioses know I'm not!*

He was the first to admit it. His last relationship hadn't lasted long, his novia eventually got fed up with canceled plans, animal hair all over his (and then her) clothing, and the steady stream of four-legged patients he brought home with him for extra supervision. Though the straw that broke the llama's back, as it were, ended up being a patient without any legs at all. But in Dario's defense, the snake had seemed very sick when he brought her home, and he certainly hadn't expected her to break out of her cage and find her way into their bed.

While Dario and his novia were sleeping in it.[1]

So no, he was well aware that no one was perfect, least of all him. Still, maybe the beautiful woman, *Asiri*, he reminded himself, just needed a chance to get to know how adorable Pepe could be.

"Don't worry, he doesn't bite!" Dario told her, as reassuringly as he could.

"Squee! Squee!" Pepe agreed. Dario patted him on the head. *Good boy,* he thought. *Keep being a sweetheart.*

"He broke two of his legs, poor guy," Dario continued, "and I can't leave him at my facilities in town. He chews through his bindings and makes things worse for himself."

Asiri stared stiffly at Pepe as he continued his gentle chirping.

---

1. In Dario's defense, that particular snake was not, in fact, venomous.

"So, the village is not far?" Asiri asked, jerking her gaze from Pepe and back at him. Dario did his best to not stare, but it was difficult. She really was so lovely.

"Yes! It's not far," he told her, happy to help. "So, if you continue following the river, you will reach some fishing huts, which won't be used right now. Our fisherman split the year between ocean and river fishing, depending on the season."

Pepe chirped and grunted, and Dario noticed that Asiri's eyes kept flicking between him and the cuy. Did the guinea pig really make her that nervous?

"But eventually, you will reach the main stretch of downtown Pisqu. You can take that straight to the coast, if that's where you're headed! Unless you were looking for the inn? Because that is closer to the town center, which you can also reach from the coast, but you need to do a little loop."

"Wheek! Wheek!" Pepe interjected. Dario patted his head before continuing.

"But actually, if you want to reach the main square, what you could do is just follow the river until you hit some dirt paths, follow those, and when they turn to stone roads, you will know you are going in the right direction."

"Ya, cállate!" Asiri snapped, and Dario stopped speaking immediately.[2] Embarrassment burned in the center of his chest, and he did his best not to duck his head. It wasn't the first time he had spoken too much to a stranger. The poor girl was soaking wet, most likely cold, and all she wanted was to get to Pisqu. There had

---

2. "Cállate" means be quiet/stop talking/shut up. Oops.

been no need to talk her ear off, but Dario found himself too busy trying to impress her.

Tonto, he chastised himself.

"No, I didn't mean—"" Asiri began, but Dario waved her off.

"No, no, you're right, I do tend to talk too much. You are probably anxious to get on your way." He backed up from her quickly, not wanting to waste any more of her time.

"No, really," she started, but Dario interrupted her.

"Perhaps we will see one another again in Pisqu," he blurted. He didn't want her to feel bad for rushing him along. She was absolutely right. And as loath as he was to leave her presence, he would pray to the dioses that he would see her again in Pisqu. With a small bow, he continued deeper into the forest to pick the medicinal herbs he was there for. Disappointment and shame made his chest hot, and he could feel his shoulders slump.

Pepe squeaked at him comfortingly, and Dario patted him again. "Gracias Pepe, I love you too, buddy."

DOVE/
PALOMA

CHAPTER 7

ASIRI

T he hummingbird shook out its feathers and then locked eyes with Asiri.

"That did *not* go well," he told her, and Asiri couldn't help but agree.

She had tried to focus on Dario's words. She truly had! But the horrible Marco kept interrupting her and slinging obscenities her way. When Dario had promised that the cuy did not bite, the animal became enraged.

"I most certainly *do* bite! Get those fingers close to me and I will prove it to you, you horrible human!" the guinea pig had screeched. As Dario tried to give her directions to Pisqu, it only got worse.

"Release me, or I will find a way to crawl into your bedroom at night and nibble off your toes! I will eat your hair! I will leave pellets in your bed!" Marco had howled. "I will gouge out your eyes with my claws! I will hide all your undergarments!"

Finally, Asiri had had enough and told him to shut up. It just slipped out of her, annoyance making her careless. Of course, Dario thought she spoke to him, and it wasn't like she could explain without confessing the truth of her gift. She had just had to stand there, mortification coursing through her veins as the handsome animal healer walked away.

An animal healer! Asiri sighed longingly. *He is an animal healer!* Someone who not only loved and appreciated animals the way that she did, but knew how to help them, how to fix their wounds and mend their hurts. How many times had she wished that she could help her friends in that way? Asiri, of all people, could know exactly what was ailing them. But to be able to aid in their recovery? That was miraculous.

With another sigh, Asiri resolved to handle her gift better around people. It was always difficult ignoring animals when they were speaking directly to her, but she was sure it would get easier.

The hummingbird, whose name was Felipe, kept watch while she changed out of her wet clothes. When she emerged, he flitted up to perch on her right shoulder, and she continued towards what she hoped would be her new home. Felipe hadn't said as much—he hadn't said much of anything since his ordeal in the water—but it seemed that he was determined to stay with Asiri for a while longer.

Little by little, they made their way closer to civilization. The first hints were some abandoned fisherman's huts that lined the river. Then, the distant sounds of people speaking. Eventually, Asiri passed by a small group of children playing amongst the wildflowers that lined the riverbank. Finally, they were in the town of Pisqu.

Pisqu appeared divided in two, half of the houses and buildings on one side of the river, and the other half on the opposite bank. A tangle of wooden and rope paths connected the two sides with gently arched bridges. People were happily crossing to and from each section, milling about the stone pathways that lined either side of the banks. There were restaurants and tienditas, people coming in and out of buildings, buying wares, and spilling out into the streets.

The colors were overwhelming, shades of pinks, yellows, teals, and soft grays, reflected in paintings, murals, clothing, and decor. Asiri had never experienced so much vibrance and life. The towns and villages in the mountains tended to reflect more earthen-colored tones and simpler patterns. It was rare to see any colors besides black and gold in the Casa de Murmuros. But clearly these coastal people had a love for all things bright and cheery, and the sight of it lifted Asiri's heart.

As she made her way towards what looked like a bustling town square, new and varied smells assaulted her nose. The flowers that grew on the sides of the river were sweet and fragrant, but the vendor stalls in the center square sold salty-smelling fish and other marine life that Asiri had never witnessed before. There were plump and juicy cuts of fruits that held citrusy and syrupy notes. She could smell pan, chocolate, cafe and spices.

But as she wandered, carefree and aimless, there was one scent that cut through the rest. It was sweet and buttery, rich and decadent. The smell promised her the best mouthful of food that she had ever experienced in her life, and her stomach rumbled hungrily in anticipation. Ignoring the curious stares sent in her direction, Asiri inhaled deeply, trying to locate the source of the mouth-watering aroma. She followed the gently wafting scent to a small storefront, its pink window shutters thrown wide open;

releasing the heavenly smell. Above the open and inviting door hung a pink and teal wooden sign that read "Paloma's Pastries."[1]

Felipe tucked himself behind her hair as Asiri walked into the establishment. There were a few small tables and chairs on the sides of the wide rectangular room, but a long, wooden bar overflowing with fat, decadent looking pastries and sweets occupied much of the space. Behind them all was a short, plump woman who looked to be about Asiri's age. Her skin was more golden than Asiri's bronze, and where Asiri's dark hair fell straight down like a waterfall, this woman's locks cascaded over her shoulders like thick, reddish brown ocean waves, constantly in motion. She was wearing a pink and teal apron and, on her full cheeks, a smattering of flour mixed with her freckles.

"Hola, hola!" she called out to Asiri, motioning her towards the bar. Asiri complied, sitting on one of the tall stools in front of her.

"I'm Paloma," the woman told her with a smile so wide the edges of her eyes crinkled. Then she leaned forward and whispered, "and I have a gift."

Asiri startled, jerking back in her chair. She felt Felipe buzz in protest behind her ear.

A gift? An ability? All the way out here? Had she not just traveled the better part of a month to get away from the Casa and all the people with gifts?

With her shock also came confusion. Asiri's gift had always met with distrust outside of the tall walls of the Casa de Murmuros. Everywhere she went, people greeted her with wary suspicion. It didn't matter that she travelled town to town fulfilling the tasks

---

1. "Paloma" means "dove."

those same townspeople asked of her. Still, the people always viewed her as a suspicious outsider. Which was one of the main reasons Asiri was so determined to not let anyone in her new town discover her ability. For this woman to announce that she had a gift so publicly— and shamelessly—was a novelty.

"My gift," Paloma continued, winking conspiratorially, "is that I can tell just what a person wants to eat, sometimes, even before they do!"

Asiri felt her shoulders relax. That didn't sound like the sort of "gift" that the people of her old home possessed. Perhaps it was simply a sales tactic?

"That seems like a very useful gift for someone who owns a pastelería," Asiri admitted, and Paloma laughed.

"You don't seem to believe me," the woman said, her smile never dimming. "But I'm about to prove it to you."

Paloma walked the long length of the wooden table, picking up certain dishes, and then setting them down again. Asiri's mouth watered as Paloma lingered by a platter of alfajores, the thin, buttery cookies sandwiching a thick layer of dulce de leche in their centers. Paloma continued past them, and Asiri couldn't help but lean in to watch the woman's progress. Paloma disregarded the chocolate section, spent a few seconds over the bread, but then shook her head. Her smile remained, but a small crinkle creased the skin between her brows. Finally, she straightened and beamed at Asiri.

"I've got it!" she said, grabbing a flat blade and cutting a piece of flaky pastry covered with fruit. "This is a tartaleta de fruta," she explained, setting the plate in front of Asiri with a flourish. Handing her a napkin and fork, Paloma crossed her arms, leaned her elbows on the wooden bar, and waited for Asiri to take the first bite.

Still a bit skeptical, Asiri lifted the fork and speared a generous portion. Bringing it to her mouth, she slid the pastry past her lips. When it hit her tongue, her eyes widened in surprise. Then a groan of pleasure escaped her, which made Paloma chuckle.

The pastry crust was buttery and rich, crumbling daintily into flaky pieces around her teeth. The whipped, creamy center was decadent, thick, and rich. The sugary sweetness of it slid across the top of her tongue. Finally, the crisp, slightly acidic bite of the fruit on top rounded out the dessert with the perfect combination of flavors.

"I should never have doubted your gift," Asiri admitted to Paloma, cramming her mouth with another forkful.

Laughing, Paloma gave her a small bow, flourishing her arms to the sides. "So, tell me," she said when she straightened. "What brings you to Pisqu?"

Asiri felt herself flush. "Is it that obvious that I'm not from around here?" she asked, fiddling with the hem of her shirt.

"It's a small town," Paloma shrugged. "And I've lived here my entire life, so I'm pretty familiar with our residents. Besides, even if I wasn't, all that travel equipment might have clued me in," she said as she jerked her chin in the direction of Asiri's discarded bags.

Asiri couldn't help but laugh. In her utter delight of the fruit tart, she had completely forgotten that all her earthly belongings lay scattered around her on the clean wooden floor.

"I just wanted a fresh start," Asiri answered Paloma honestly. "And something led me to the coast."

"Have you seen the ocean yet?" Paloma asked with a twinkle in her eye.

Asiri paused for just a second, then answered, "Not yet."

It was true, in a sense. She had only encountered it in her spirit form, not her corporeal body. She was looking forward to the experience.

Paloma's eyes brightened. "You're going to love it," she promised.

"Paloma," Asiri said, after swallowing another perfect bite of sugary delight. "Do you happen to know of anyone who is offering work?" she asked. "I'll do anything, truly!"

Paloma cocked her head and pursed her lips, her eyes squinting contemplatively. After a moment, she snapped her fingers.

"Dario, our animal healer is looking for an assistant! He always needs help with the amount of creatures that man rescues. He can never say no to an animal in need, whether he has space for them or not. Somehow, he always finds a way, and the time, but the poor man is run ragged. He really needs someone who can help!"

Asiri flushed cold, and the last bit of flaky crust turned to ash in her mouth. In another world, it would have been the perfect job for her. Being able to tell someone exactly what ailed their furry companions, and then be able to help.

But currently, it was impossible. The last thing Asiri wanted was for anyone to guess her ability, and if anyone could do it, it was the charismatic animal healer. Besides, her first encounter with the man hadn't exactly painted her in the best light. She dreaded running into him again.

Liar, a voice in her head whispered, conjuring an image of his hands cupped around hers while she held Felipe. At the memory of the touch, butterflies erupted in her belly.

"Oh," she fumbled awkwardly. "The thing is, with animals ..."

"You're not an animal person?" Paloma inferred with an understanding nod of her head. "That's all right, my mother isn't either. I understand."

Asiri didn't correct her. It was easier than trying to come up with a lie that would keep her gift a secret.

"Let me see." Paloma adopted the same look as before, eyes squinted, brows pinched, finger tapping on her chin. Then she brightened.

"I know!" she exclaimed. "You can go to Doña Iris!"[2]

"Doña Iris?" Asiri repeated, straightening in her chair.

Paloma nodded furiously. "She is a weaver and has a shop where she works absolute wonders with her loom. She dyes all the cotton yarn herself, but she is getting older and her hands are not quite what they used to be. I'm sure she could use some help!"

"That sounds perfect!" Asiri said, the light of her excitement burning away the nerves that had settled in her after hearing Dario's name.

Paloma gave Asiri directions on where to find Doña Iris's shop, "Tienda del Tejido" and made her promise to meet her for dinner

---

2. "Doña" is a feminine prefix meaning "Madam" or "Lady."

at the local tavern not far from Paloma's Pastries.[3] She refused to accept payment for the tartaleta de fruta—a welcome gift, she called it—and sent Asiri out the door with renewed purpose and a fat butter cookie.

Asiri found the tienda without too much trouble and stopped at its threshold to wipe the crumbs off her mouth and straighten her clothing. With a fortifying breath, she walked inside.

It was spectacular. Yarn and fabric covered every surface of the shop. The entire store looked as if someone had harnessed a rainbow, and its colors erupted in an explosion of tones and shades within the room. The patterns were overwhelming and the attention to detail sublime.

Asiri reached out to touch a particularly fine-looking yard of cloth when a pointed cough sounded behind her. Dropping her hand, Asiri spun to see a very short, severe-looking woman scowling at her. Asiri couldn't tell her age, she could have been anywhere between fifty and eighty years old. Her hair, which was liberally streaked with gray and white, was braided and then coiled into a tight bun on the top of her head, pulling at the corners of her already slanted eyes. Eyes that were knotted with experience, but also glaring daggers at Asiri.

"Oh! Hola," Asiri said, resisting the urge to step backwards. "Are you Doña Iris?"

"Who else would I be?" the woman asked her, the scowl remaining. "It's my store, isn't it?"

---

3. Directly translated, "Tienda del Tejido" means "shop of fabrics," but the more accurate translation in this instance would be "shop of the weaving arts."

Asiri blinked, taken aback by the woman's curt demeanor. "Well," she continued, "my name is Asiri. I am new to Pisqu and am looking for a job. Paloma, from Paloma's Pastries? She mentioned you might have work for me."

Doña Iris's shoulders relaxed. "Ah, Miguel's girl sent you? I suppose that's all right then." She shuffled towards the far end of the building, and Asiri followed her, hoping that was what the older woman intended. They reached the back of the store, where they both ducked under a braided curtain.

Asiri gasped. It was some sort of storage room, except every bit of wall space held shelves, which contained all manner of flowers, powders, dead insects, and other items she could not identify.

"What is all this?" Asiri couldn't help but ask.

"How do you think clothes get their color?" Doña Iris demanded, then looked at Asiri's plain black travel clothes and scoffed. "Well, not your clothes, ugly things that they are. But most clothes?"

Asiri's cheeks burned with embarrassment. She knew she looked terribly drab compared to the older woman, with her pumpkin orange shawl, decorated in an egg-yolk-yellow sun pattern. Underneath, she had a long tunic in a complementary terracotta color. A thick golden belt and long necklace of gold completed the woman's outfit.

Asiri thought she looked beautiful.

"I don't know how clothes get their colors," Asiri admitted. "They are dyed?"

"Of course they are dyed," Doña Iris replied. "But dyed with what?"

Asiri's eyes grew wide with understanding. She gestured around her. "With these materials? With plants and flowers?"

"And more," Doña Iris said with a nod. She lifted a woven stretch of purple fabric and passed it to Asiri. "That color can be made by mashing those caracoles over there," she motioned to a pile of sea snails. "And there are some bugs inside of certain cacti that, when ground up and boiled, create red," she continued, motioning to bright crimson woolen threads hanging over a drying line.

The older woman shuffled to a shelf and pulled out a light bluish-purple plant. "When picked on a regular day, this plant will dye the yarn a cyan color," she explained. "But if picked under a full moon, it creates a deep midnight blue pigment."

"No way!" Asiri gasped, amazed. "Truly?"

Doña Iris's eyes twinkled, and for the first time, the woman looked almost friendly. "Truly," she said, handing Asiri the flower.

"Wow," she replied, delicately turning it over in her fingers. Then she looked down at her drab clothing with a frown. "What about black?" she asked, more out of curiosity. She was interested, despite never wanting to wear the dark color again!

Doña Iris looked at her disapprovingly. "You get fleece from a black sheep or alpaca."

"Oh," Asiri mumbled, mortified.

Of course. Obviously. What a dumb question!

"There are countless materials found in nature which can create the beauty you see around you," Doña Iris said. "If you only know where to look. The problem is ..." she sighed. "I am not as young as I once was. My fingers still work for the loom, you see, but if I spend most of my day out in the woods collecting materials, well," she said with a shrug. "I tire more quickly than I used to."

"I can help!" Asiri volunteered quickly. "If you show me what to gather, and where to go, I can collect the materials for you!" she said, almost giddy with excitement. It would be wonderful work. She loved being out in nature, and maybe if she did a good enough job, eventually Doña Iris would teach her how she made all those lovely fabrics and clothes!

Doña Iris squinted at her. "Do you have anywhere to stay, niña?" she asked her.

Asiri's excitement dimmed. She didn't. Would that be a problem?

"Well, no, not yet," she admitted. "But I don't mind sleeping in the woods, really! And once I make a little money, I'm sure I can find a place to rent!"

"My house is a few streets from here, away from the town center," Doña Iris said. "But this store has a room above the main building, with stairs outside that lead to it. It doesn't have much, but you can have it while you work for me."

Shocked, tears prickled the backs of Asiri's eyes. "Gracias, muchísimas gracias!"

"Just work hard, and that will be thanks enough," Doña Iris replied, moving back to the front of the shop. "Come, I will show you to your new home."

MACAW/
GUACAMAYA

CHAPTER 8

ASIRI

That evening Asiri made her way to the local taverna to meet Paloma as promised. When she arrived, she found that the woman was not there yet, but as the signage above the door promised it to be the correct location, "Mama Qucha's Cocina," she decided not to worry.[1]

"Do you want to come inside with me?" she asked Felipe quietly. The tiny bird still perched on her shoulder, hidden by her hair, and she felt him shift.

"You can stay with me," she was quick to reassure him. "But there is a lovely bush of flowers just ahead, if you wanted to wait outside."

A breeze rustled her hair as Felipe flapped his wings and emerged from their dark curtain. "I will meet you when you come back out!" he promised, before flitting towards the flowers.

---

1. Mama Qucha is the feminine Inca goddess of the sea. She is the patron goddess of sailors and fishermen, goddess of marine life, and revered by coastal people for her influence. "Cocina" means kitchen.

Inside the taverna, Asiri found a wooden floor instead of a stone one, and a large fireplace that stretched upwards on the far side of the long rectangular room. It was not lit, but held a few short, fat candles that illuminated the area with a faint, buttery glow. Asiri allowed herself to imagine what the room must look like in the winter, when it was lit with a roaring fire, crackling and sputtering on a cold night, the warmth of it comforting sailors and shopkeepers alike as they joined under this roof for a hot, hearty meal and a strong drink.

Asiri made her way towards the long bar, needing to dodge and weave past the throngs of patrons as she did so. The hour was getting late, so there were many customers, people finishing out their days with good meals and even better company.

When she finally managed to reach the bar, she noted with relief that there were three empty stools in a row. She sat herself on one nearest an open window, where she could see the sun already disappearing shyly behind the horizon.

As Asiri looked around the room, a small thrill rushed through her chest. She had dined alone in other tavernas in different villages over the years, as her assignments from Casa de Murmuros often required travel, but her presence in those towns never went unnoticed. "She's one of them," people would whisper. "A gifted one. Different. Dangerous."

In Mama Qucha's Cocina, she could just *be*. There were no suspicious stares or distrustful murmurs making her shoulders tense and belly churn. She could enjoy an evening meal as a regular person. And with a potential new friend!

The bartender, a sweet-faced, floppy-haired young man with a friendly smile, noticed her after a few moments, and pointed to a menu behind him which already had several items crossed off.

"We are out of the lomo saltado," he told her while wiping the wood in front of her with a sage green towel, "and the seco de cordero. But we have a seafood stew, and we can do mariscos saltados instead. We never run out of seafood out here!" he told her with a wink that was more friendly than flirtatious. Asiri blushed anyway, unused to the attention.

"I'm meeting someone," she told him. "I'll wait to order when she arrives."

"Of course," he said, and slid over a tall glass of cerveza. "While you wait," he told her. "On the house, and welcome to Pisqu!"

Asiri shook her head. What was it about these people that made them want to give her food and drink for free? Whatever it was, she certainly wouldn't complain about it, since she still did not have much moneda to spend. Still, she wondered if all the people on the coast were as kind as the ones she had met so far. Even Doña Iris, who had seemed brusque and cold, had helped her more than she could have imagined! Remembering that she had secured not only a job, but a place to stay on her first day in the village, she couldn't help but burst into a wide grin behind the rim of her glass.

"You seem in a much better mood than earlier," a voice said to her as they slipped onto the third barstool, leaving the chair between them empty.

Asiri jerked her head up, beer foam tickling the skin above her top lip. She was both surprised and thrilled to find that it was Dario, looking just as tempting as he had by the river. Hastily, she swiped at her mouth with the back of her hand and straightened up on the stool.

"I'm so sorry about earlier," she blurted. "I just—" she looked down and noticed that the temperamental guinea pig was no longer with him. Relieved, she met his eyes. "I think I was in shock from jumping into the water."

"No need to apologize," Dario said with a grin, and Asiri noticed that he had a single dimple in his right cheek. Her heartbeat fluttered in her throat. "How did the colibrí make out? Was he all right?" he asked.

"Yes," Asiri replied happily. "He was a little stunned for a while, but then was perfectly fine. Thankfully."

"He was lucky that you were there," Dario said, leaning forward.

The muscles underneath his tunic shifted with his movements, and Asiri felt dizzy. Was it the beer? She glanced at her glass, still mostly full of cerveza. Nope, couldn't blame it on the beer.

"Most people wouldn't have jumped into a river to save an animal like that," he continued.

"You would have," Asiri guessed.

"I would have," he agreed softly, and they shared a smile. Asiri watched as his eyes scanned her face, and she felt his gaze like a caress. Flushed, she sat back in her chair.

"I have to ask," Asiri said, eager to keep the conversation going. "Why was there so much rope above the river? I saw it as far out as we were, and it stretched all the way to the town. Here it's all decorated with hanging lanterns and pretty streamers, but why extend it so far?"

"You've never heard of Amaru deterrents?" Dario asked, seeming surprised.

"Amarus?" Asiri repeated, confused. "The semidioses of water?" she barked out a nervous laugh.[2] "They are just folktales, they aren't real!"

"Aren't they?" Dario asked thoughtfully.

"Of course not!" Asiri insisted. "They are simply tales that we tell to children, to make them cautious around water. There aren't really winged part-llama, part-fish, part-snake creatures out there!"

Dario shrugged. "Just because we haven't seen one doesn't mean that they don't exist. Being so close to the coast, this town can't afford to have an angry semidios nearby. Especially not one that can control the water."

"So, all the rope, they are traps?" Asiri asked, stunned.

"Deterrents," Dario clarified. "To keep the creature from venturing too far from the river. The people are afraid of the semidios's curse. We would rather it stay far away." Dario smiled at her. "If it exists, of course."

"Of course," Asiri answered, a little dazed. In her time traveling from village to village, she had met many superstitious people, many religious people, people with their own customs, rituals, and beliefs. But she had never found a town who all believed in a folktale! Still, she wasn't about to judge the people of her new home.

"So, what brings you to Pisqu?" Dario asked, as if reading her mind. Just then, with the absolute worst timing, a group of blue

2. "Semidios" means "demigod."

and gold macaws landed on the tree outside of the window Asiri was sitting next to.

"This is the one! This is the one!" she heard one of them screech. "This is the human who can speak to us! I saw her earlier, speaking to a colibrí!"

Distracted, Asiri shook her head, trying to keep her attention on Dario.

"I'm sorry, what did you say?" she asked him.

"Hey! Hey, señorita, throw us some food!" a voice outside the window called out.

"Yeah, we're starving!" another one said.

"I just asked what brought you to Pisqu," Dario repeated.

"Oh, I just wanted a fresh start and a change," Asiri began, only to be interrupted again.

"Come on señorita, don't be stingy!" The first macaw yelled at her, perching on the edge of the windowsill.

"And I love the ocean," Asiri tried to continue, doing her best to ignore the birds behind her.

"So, you've been to the ocean before? Did you live in another coastal town?" Dario asked.

"Hey, señorita, is that man your boyyyyfriend?" one of the parrots teased with a singsong tone.

"What? No, of course not," Asiri snapped out irritably.

Dario sat back in his chair, looking offended.

"I'm sorry, I didn't mean to assume," he started.

"No! No, I just meant—No, I have never been to the ocean before," she stammered, trying to shut out the ruckus and listen only to Dario. Unfortunately, the macaws were loud!

He sent her a tentative smile. "Then how do you know that you love it?" he asked, his voice teasing.

"*Do* you have a boyfriend?" the same parrot asked, hopping right behind her left elbow and pecking it with his beak.

"That's none of your business," she tried to whisper while nudging the bird away, but Dario heard her anyway. He swiveled in his chair to face forward, no longer looking at her.

"Of course," he replied stiffly.

"I—"" Asiri started, wanting to assure him that she hadn't intended any offense, and hopefully save the conversation. But before she could continue, she stopped herself.

If Asiri was being honest, she knew it would be better to not get any closer to the animal healer. She should just let the man think that she was rude and horrible. It was better than him thinking she was crazy, and infinitely better than him finding out her secret. This was for the best. She should be happy that he no longer wished to speak with her.

But Asiri didn't feel happy. She felt miserable.

Luckily for her, at that moment, Paloma finally arrived and took her seat between Asiri and Dario. She greeted Dario with a quick hello, which the animal healer returned with a much warmer disposition than he had just a moment ago. Asiri did her best not to take it personally.

Then Paloma turned her attention to Asiri.

"Well?" Paloma asked. "How did it go with Doña Iris?"

"Don't ignore us! We know you can hear us!" the first bird squawked at her again.

"Hold that thought," Asiri told Paloma, before turning around and shutting the window. The night had grown dark anyway, and the bar was well lit with candles. The window no longer needed to be open. She could still make out the muffled protests of the noxious birds through the glass and wood, but were soft enough that Asiri could easily ignore them.

I should have done that sooner, she thought.

"It went wonderfully," Asiri finally answered Paloma. "She gave me a job!"

Paloma squealed. "Oh, my dioses, that's amazing! I knew she could use the help!" She threw her arms around Asiri, who returned the hug with both gratitude and pure joy.

"Thank you so much for helping me!" she told Paloma.

Dario, who was unabashedly listening to their conversation, leaned around Paloma.

"If she needed a job, why didn't you send her to me? You know that I'm looking for help!"

Asiri peeked at his face, noting that he looked more hurt than annoyed.

"Asiri doesn't like animals," Paloma told him, shoving at his shoulder.

Dario's brows furrowed, and he looked at Asiri in confusion. "But—" he started, before Paloma interrupted him.

"It's not a crime, Dario! Not everyone likes animals as much as you do!" she said.

"Of course, I know that," he replied, but he continued to regard Asiri curiously. "It's just that, at the river—"

Before he could finish his statement, a large, dark hand clasped him over the shoulder. Asiri looked up and found a whirling tempest of a man attached to that hand, intimidating and dangerous looking, but impossible to glance away from. His hair was as dark as Dario's, but where the animal healer had soft waves, this man's thick locks sat closely cropped to his head. His brows were heavy and arched, low in the center of his face and sweeping high up towards his temples as if locked in a permanent scowl. His eyes were black and piercing, narrow and slanted above high cheekbones. Full lips that should've been inviting twisted into a sneer. Even so, he was beautiful, in a dark, mysterious sort of way. In fact, the only thing that marred his otherwise perfect face was the slight deviation of his nose, which indicated a break at some point.

"You're not bothering Palomita, are you, Dario?" the man asked. Somehow, he made his tone sound friendly, while still disguising the icy threat behind the words.

"Oh, stop it, Paqari! You know Dario is just a friend," Paloma said irritably, glaring up at him.

The man named Paqari ignored her.

"Just remember that she's Miguel's girl," Paqari said, tightening his grip on Dario's shoulder. To his credit, the animal healer didn't even wince.

"I know, Paqari. Don't worry." Dario replied evenly.

"I never worry," Paqari said, before turning around and making his way through the crowded taverna.

"Bye to you too!" Paloma called out, glaring at his retreating back.

Asiri regarded Paloma hesitantly, but didn't feel like she knew the woman well enough to ask about the situation outright. Still, the curiosity must have shown in her face, because Paloma rolled her eyes and said, "Long story."

Dropping it, she and Paloma ordered their meals and spent the rest of the evening talking about anything and everything. Asiri told her as much as she could about her old life without giving too much away, and Paloma filled her in on life in Pisqu. She was so thoroughly delighted with the prospect of having her first true friend that she almost didn't notice when Dario got up and left the taverna.

Almost.

Her heart dropped into her stomach when he stood, and she instinctively straightened in her chair. But he didn't even glance her way before paying for his meal and leaving.

Which was fine. Asiri was fine. The twisting in her stomach was just the result of such rich food. Definitely not disappointment.

Before she and Paloma knew it, it was late, and most of the other patrons had left the establishment as well. The bartender—whose name was Julio—began cleaning tables and stacking chairs, and the women moved to make their way home as well.

"Wait a minute Paloma, and I'll walk you home," Julio called out as they started towards the door.

"Julito, I'm perfectly capable of walking myself home!" Paloma protested.

"It's what Miguel would want," Julio said simply, and Asiri watched as Paloma deflated.

"Who is—" Asiri started, but Paloma shook her head.

"Long story, remember?" she said. "You go ahead. There'll be hell to pay if I leave without him. I'll see you tomorrow?"

Asiri's heart lifted in her chest, and the discomfort in her tummy faded. "See you tomorrow," her new friend's words echoed in her heart. She was staying here. This was her home. Asiri would see her Paloma tomorrow. She felt so fortunate.

"Hasta mañana!" Asiri replied, then slipped out into the cool night breeze. As soon as she was outside, Felipe flew out from the flower bush, and hovered in front of her face, his wings a blur by his sides. "Don't worry, Asiri, I'll take you home!" the hummingbird chirped.

Asiri smiled as he settled back on her shoulder.

"Gracias, amigo."

CHIMÚ/ PERUVIAN HAIRLESS DOG

CHAPTER 9

DARIO

The rising sun was just peeking over the horizon, the warming rays caressing Dario's face through the open window. Smiling, he rubbed his hand over his thick black hair, then patted it down as best he could before swinging his feet off the bed. He checked the floor before setting them down on the wood, however, as he had a habit of bringing some of his patients home with him and didn't want to step on any little paw or fuzzy body. Seeing that the coast was clear, he stood up and stretched, going through his list of things to do today.

First things first. He checked on the elderly guinea pig that had become a constant companion for him in the last few weeks. If he was being honest with himself, Dario appreciated the company. Even though he found himself constantly surrounded by people and patients, returning to his empty house at night could get rather lonely. Even when he brought some of the more injured or sick animals home with him, those nights were usually sleepless and filled with worry. But since Pepe was in no immediate danger and just needed extra supervision, Dario had an excuse to be accompanied, and found he liked the experience.

There was, of course, another's company he would have preferred.

As he got ready for the day, washing up and cleaning his teeth, Dario couldn't help thinking about the evening before and seeing Asiri again. Before entering Julio's taverna, he had almost convinced himself that he had made up their entire encounter, or that, at the very least, he was exaggerating her beauty in his head. Surely, no mortal woman could be as lovely as the memory he had of Asiri.

But then he walked into the bar and saw her, the setting sun stroking her dark hair and bathing her face in light. She'd left him breathless, and he couldn't understand why every eye in the establishment wasn't upon her. He hadn't thought, but crossed instinctively to her as quickly as he could, his heart in his throat until he could secure the empty seat near her.

At first, all seemed well. She had smiled at him. He felt the warmth of it even still. They had chatted for a few moments and the hope that flooded Dario's chest threatened to drown him. But then, everything about her demeanor had changed, from one moment to another, and Dario just knew that somehow, he had messed up again. Had he been bothering her? Asiri was brand new to Pisqu, and there he was, bombarding her with his presence and his questions.

Dario shook his head. When would he learn?

Ever since he was young, people told him that he came on too strong, that he was too loud, too animated, too passionate. *Too much*. He was always spouting off random facts about animals, sneaking frogs and lizards into his home, or bringing squirrels into school. Over the years, he had played "the quiet game" more times than he could count, been told to "hush," to "calm down," to "settle." He'd confused and frustrated his parents. His teachers despaired at his lack of attention in classrooms. Friends had tired of his energy, and girls had thought him too strange to date.

Dario had worked very hard over the years to rein himself in. To make himself quieter, more reserved, less excitable. He stifled the urge to talk at length about things that he was interested in and passionate about. And it worked! He had started making friends, had started dating, people began respecting him in his profession. He had carved out a good life for himself, and the distracted, impulsive kid people thought of as "too much" faded into a distant memory. But every now and then, that side of him would reemerge, leaving Dario feeling vulnerable and embarrassed.

"I must have talked too much again last night," he said out loud to Pepe as he secured him into his little sling. The guinea pig chuffed, and together they walked out onto the street. Dario's small house was only a few blocks away from his practice, and he nodded politely or waved at the few townspeople who were on their way to their own jobs. When he arrived, he unlocked the front door, opened all the windows (which were covered in thin gauzy nets lest a winged patient accidentally get free) and went to check on his overnight residents.

Currently, Dario was treating a tiny piglet. The runt of the litter, whose mother rejected it, and because of the little guy's size, he wasn't able to feed properly, as his brothers and sisters kept nudging him out of the way before he could reach the teat. Dario knew that when mothers rejected their young, there were usually internal issues at play that the mother was more aware of than he.

But so far, the piglet responded well to regular feedings and his warm, comfy cage, so Dario wasn't giving up hope.

After he fed and cleaned the piglet, he moved on to Lorenzo the lizard. Lorenzo was a lava lizard and the pet of a young boy named Eduardo. The boy's parents brought him in after Lorenzo had seemed lethargic and lifeless. When the family returned today, Dario would let them know that Lorenzo was a bit malnourished. They needed to start feeding him fewer vegetables and more insects. After a steady diet of flies and beetles, Lorenzo already appeared much more lively.

Dario made the rounds, giving each animal as much care and attention as they needed, before making his way to the back office. He left Pepe in his cage—the cuy would be all right for a few minutes—before opening the door.

A flash of blue-gray collided against his body, toppling Dario to the floor. Once down, his face was thoroughly bathed in big, slobbery dog kisses. Dario laughed, sitting up, cuddling the enormous pup to his side.

Dario had found the chimú dog several days prior.[1] Despite her large size, Dario noted that she was still just a puppy, barely a year old. She was, like most dogs of her breed, completely hairless except for the small patch of fuzz on her head and on her tail. The same tail that was whipping back and forth so hard, Dario was afraid that he would have a bruise on his back by the time they were done with the examination.

"All right, girl, settle down now," he said, which only made the dog lift her oversized paws onto Dario's shoulders and attempt to

---

1. Chimú dogs are also known as Peruvian hairless dogs.

attack his face with kisses once more. Dario did his best to remain professional, but when the dog began nibbling on his ear instead, he couldn't help but roar with laughter once again.

Dario had found the puppy in a small cove near the beach, severely dehydrated and overheated. Because chimú dogs do not have fur, prolonged exposure to the sun can be very dangerous to them. Dario had carried her to the practice and did everything he could for her, his worry chipping away piece after piece of his heart until he was finally sure that the pup would pull through.

Once she had, Dario had fallen in love with the girl. Dario cared for all the animals that passed through his practice, but there was something about this dog that he couldn't deny. She still had some skin conditions that needed to be treated, but would be fine in about a week or so. Dario knew it was a possibility that the pup could have previous owners who could stop in his practice looking for her, and Dario was prepared to let her go if that was the case. (As long as her getting out and becoming sick from the heat had been an accident, of course. He would never judge a good pet parent over an accident.) But a not-so-small, selfish part of him hoped that no one ever came, and that he could take the chimú home with him.

After Dario finished rubbing balsam oil over the dog's scaly heat rashes, she settled on the cool floor with her head in Dario's lap. She gazed adoringly up at Dario, her big chocolate eyes wide and trusting. Dario gently scratched her head as her tail swished over the ground.

"Can you keep a secret, linda?" Dario asked her, and her tail wagged faster.

Dario smiled and leaned his head against the wall.

"I met a girl."

MOUSE/
RATONCITO

CHAPTER 10

ASIRI

"Asiri! Asiri! Time to wake up!"

Asiri slowly opened her eyes, squinting against the rising sun which was carving a narrow path between the crack in her blinds and the bed.

My bed, she thought, stretching with a happy smile.

Her room above the Tienda de Tejidos looked sparsely furnished, but for the time being, it was hers. A simple, single bed rested against the wall, but the blanket on top held a colorful array of happy pinks, yellows, purples, and blues that striped across it. There was a woven rectangular rug with an embroidered diamond pattern in complimentary colors in the room's center, a small round table, and two squat, fat stools. When she had returned the evening prior, she'd found that Doña Iris left a cluster of lilies in a bumblebee-colored vase on the windowsill, and Asiri nearly cried at the gesture. The space was not large, but it was clean, cheery, and colorful, and Asiri felt grateful that she would be waking up in it every morning.

"I don't mean to rush you," Felipe said politely, landing on the top of the vase and peeking out the window. "But Doña Iris is about halfway down the road already, and I don't think you'd like to be late on your first day."

Asiri flung her covers off and scrambled out of bed. She washed as quickly as she could, and threw on her travel clothes, hoping once again that soon she would be able to afford something nicer for herself. After a moment's hesitation, she fished out her mother's necklace from the top drawer of her dresser where she had placed it the night before, and fastened it around her neck. The instant the cool metal settled on her skin, she felt more steady. It was time to start her new job!

That afternoon, Asiri sat dejectedly on the dirt with her head in her hands. All the hopeful optimism that she had started the day with had evaporated hours ago.

Doña Iris had greeted her as gruffly as she had the day prior, but Asiri didn't let that bring her down. She was determined to win the woman over with her good-natured charm and work ethic. Then the older woman sent Asiri out with a large basket and vague instructions on where to find a specific type of tree in order to gather its leaves, claiming they were used to create yellow dye. Asiri had bolted out of the shop promising to return with plenty of leaves, intent on proving her worth. But after hours of trekking through the hot, humid forest with no sign of the plant in sight, she had all but given up.

"She's going to fire me," Asiri mumbled into her hands. "And kick me out of the shop. Then I won't have a job or a place to live."

"Are you all right, darling?" a small voice asked her, and Asiri glanced down to see a little field mouse standing on her hind legs to peer up at her.

"Hello," Asiri greeted her, offering her hand in case the mouse wanted to view her closer. She scrambled up onto it right away, and Asiri lifted her nearer to her face.

"Is something the matter?" the mouse asked her.

"Nothing for you to worry about, my little friend," Asiri answered, using her other hand to dig in her pocket for a handful of grapes. Her limited funds hadn't bought her much food from the mercado the day prior, but what little she had, she was happy to share. She handed one to the mouse, who began chewing on it nimbly.

"I'm Asiri. What is your name?" she asked the mouse.

"Isabella," she answered in between nibbles. "Thank you for the grapes, Asiri. Are you sure there is nothing that I can help you with?"

Asiri couldn't help but smile. "Not unless you know where I can find more of these leaves," Asiri answered, lifting the plant that Doña Iris had given her for reference.

Isabella abandoned her grape and scampered from Ariri's right hand to her left, where she was holding the leaves.

"Ah, molle tree leaves!" she said in a squeaky voice, gripping them in her little hands. "Of course, I can take you to a field full of them!"

Asiri blinked at the mouse, astonished. "Really?" she finally asked. "You know where to find these?"

Isabella nodded. "Yes, they are pink pepper trees! I don't eat the berries, but sometimes the birds do. They act funny afterwards."[1]

"Could you take me to them?" Asiri asked. "I'd be happy to give you the rest of my grapes as a thank you," she assured the small mouse.

"I would have done it anyway, but I will accept the grapes!" Isabella answered, running down her arm and back onto the forest floor. "Follow me!"

When Asiri returned to the Tienda del Tejido with a basket full of molle leaves, Doña Iris's eyes grew wide on her face.

"That is twice as much as I expected," the other woman grumbled, seemingly impressed. "You must have a keen eye. Good, that means we can get more done."

Asiri beamed at the praise, even though she knew she couldn't really take full credit for her success. Not that she would ever admit that, of course.

"Come," Doña Iris continued. "I will show you how to prepare the dyes."

The woman led Asiri to the back of the store, where the older woman had Asiri pick two more colors that she liked. Along with

---

1. Birds that eat pink peppercorns are often reported to act drunk afterwards. Cheers to them, honestly!

the yellow, Asiri also chose pink and violet. Together, the women heated the water, then got to work.

Despite her gruff nature, Doña Iris was patient in her instruction. She walked Asiri through the process of preparing each material, placing each into a different pot of hot water. Asiri's arms strained as she mixed the liquid, relieved when Doña Iris finally deemed them ready. Slowly and carefully, Asiri dropped pieces of yarn into the hot water, lifting and wringing them out with long sticks before hanging them to dry. Doña Iris explained that the yarn would have to dry fully, then the process repeated if they wanted a more vibrant hue.

When all the yarn was hanging in blushed, faded versions of their final colors, Asiri beamed at Doña Iris. No other woman had ever shown Asiri parts of her own culture like this, and it made her feel connected; not only to the older woman, but to her people and traditions. She liked to believe that if her mother had lived, she would have had more moments such as this one.

For the next few days, Asiri threw herself into settling into her new home. She was attentive and observant with Doña Iris as the older woman explained how each new dye material was powdered, pressed, boiled or treated in order to extract the pigments. And when Doña Iris sent her out to collect more ingredients, she utilized her gift to help her.

On the second day, she asked a couple of capybaras where to find the insects used for red dye, showing them a dead one for reference. They lead her to some cacti, where she could collect more than expected once again. On the fifth day, Doña Iris warned her that it would take time to gather enough sea snails, and that she would have to wake up extra early to scour the beach when the tide was low. But when she arrived, she traded a flock of egrets some crumbly bread for their help, and they swooped down and picked a whole basket full of them in record time. Asiri was back before breakfast, amazing Doña Iris.

"Well, since you have time, make your way to the forest then," she told her, handing her a fresh basket. "Look for achiote, a plant with fruit like this," she showed her a fuzzy looking red bulb, which she cracked open. "The seeds can be used to make orange dye," she explained.

After a quick stop at Paloma's Pastries to say hello to Paloma, and grab a snack, Asiri made her way back towards the forest surrounding the river. On her way, she ran into the same capybaras that she had met the other day. Their names were Bernardo and Yaya, and seemed just as happy to see her as she was them.

"Hola, hola!" Bernardo greeted her. "How did those bugs work out for you?" he asked.

"Seemed like too many bugs to me," Yaya added. "But I suppose you are bigger, and must eat more than we do!"

Asiri smiled at them, taking no offense. Animals weren't often deliberately rude, just very straightforward. There were some that tended to be more polite, like her spectacled bear friends, or more gossipy, like jacamar birds. They usually didn't mean any harm.

Then, Asiri remembered Marco, the ornery cuy.

Most animals, anyway, she thought.

"The bugs worked out wonderfully," she told the capybara couple, not bothering to try to explain that she didn't eat them at all. They wouldn't understand the concepts of dyes, or clothing, or why one would want clothing dyed. Even Felipe, though supportive of her efforts, was confused by the whole thing.

"But you already have colors," he had said, looking from the darker tan of her face to the blush of her lips, and then the lighter skin on her neck. "Maybe not as many colors as I do," he admitted, fluffing out his feathers. "But you still look beautiful!"

Which was very sweet of her little friend, currently settled in his favorite spot on her shoulder. But Asiri wanted bright, beautiful, intricately decorated tunics and dresses and scarves and shawls! And for that, she needed to do a good job for Doña Iris and make enough moneda to buy some for herself.

"Do you happen to know where I could find this fruit?" Asiri asked Bernardo and Yaya, taking out the piece of achiote Doña Iris had given her for reference. Bernardo and Yaya waddled forward, sticking out their snouts and giving the fruit a few good sniffs.

"Can't say that I do," Bernardo admitted.

Yaya cocked her head up at Asiri. "I'm not sure, but I may have smelled them growing near the river. I don't remember very well though," she admitted ruefully.

"Thank you for your help!" Asiri said, and with a quick pat to both of them, changed course and headed towards the river.

As she walked, Asiri did what she always did in the wilderness. She let her mind wander and float, not focusing too heavily on any one voice in her surroundings. Murmurs, whispers, and laughter of animals floated past her, but they all blurred into a pleasant background hum, with the occasional phrase slipping through the soft edges of her mind.

"We will need more for the pups."

"Don't stray too far south. That's where the humans are!"

"Mom! Mom! Look at me,"

"He stole it. He took it from me!"

"So good, so yummy, is there more? "

It hurts.

Asiri stopped. The last voice was faint, softer than all the ones before, and she couldn't quite make out where it had come from. Something about the voice felt different, too. Asiri was used to different types of animals, and how she heard their voices. But the last voice felt more like it was speaking in her head, not like she was hearing it with her ears. She strained to listen.

Pain. It hurts.

There it was again!

Asiri did her best to follow the voice that was not a voice.

Help me, it said a little louder.

"Where are you?" she called out, knowing it was useless. Whatever animal it was, it wouldn't know she was talking to it. *Donde estas?* she thought desperately.

Hurts, hurts, pain. Such pain, why?

It was louder now, clearer in her mind. She felt the force of it as the voice tugged her closer towards the river. As Asiri broke through a clearing, she suddenly saw it and froze in her tracks. The wicker basket fell from her hands and tumbled onto the soft grass, and her mouth fell open with a sharp gasp.

Across the riverbank was an Amaru.

CAPYBARA/ CARPINCHO

CHAPTER 11

I t was impossible, but it *was* an Amaru.

Its body was long and sinuous, thicker than a snake, more like one of the fat eels Asiri had seen at the town's Seafood Market. Its tail was decidedly fishlike, pinkish-gray scales glinting in the muted sunlight that trickled through the canopy. The creature's head was that of a llama; snout long and square. As Asiri looked into its eyes she could see that they were wide and helpless, and full of pain. When Asiri took in the Amauru's wings, she could clearly see why it was in such distress. The left wing had somehow become tangled with one of the rope traps strewn across the trees. He must've flown into it and broken his wing. Then, in the struggle to get detached, only managed to wrap himself up even worse.

Asiri winced in sympathy as she could see the tight woven fibers digging into its flesh, blood matting the surrounding feathers.

"You poor thing," she said aloud.

His head jerked up and over the rushing river, looking at her straight in the eye.

You hear me? he demanded inside her head. His voice was still odd, as if they were not speaking the same language. She could understand him, but barely.

"Yes," she answered.

This, why this? he asked, his voice laced with pain. He tried to move his wing but screeched with pain.

"Dioses," a new voice whispered from behind her.

Asiri spun around to face a bewildered and frightened-looking Dario.

"That's an Amaru," he choked out.

"Yes," Asiri answered, not sure what else to say.

"What are you doing here?" he asked her, not looking away from the semidios.

"I was trying to find achiote for Doña Iris," she explained, pointing to the discarded fruit and basket on the ground. "What are you doing here?"

"I was collecting medicinal plants and herbs for healing salves," he said. "Asiri, that's an Amaru!" he repeated.

Asiri turned her head to look back at the creature, hoping vainly that it had somehow disappeared when she wasn't watching. No such luck. He remained, glaring at both of them across the water.

"We need to go," Dario said, gripping her arm. The contact sent delicious little electric shocks shooting down Asiri's skin, but she made herself pull away.

"We can't just leave it. He's injured!" she protested.

"Asiri, it will curse us both if we stay!"

"No, it won't!" she scoffed, but internally, she wasn't so sure. She had never dealt with an Amaru before. In fact, a few days ago, she hadn't even believed that they existed! All she knew was that he was alone and in pain. She couldn't just leave.

"You're not going to curse us, are you?" she called out to the Amaru, and Dario gripped her arm again.

"Are you crazy? Don't get its attention!" he cried.

Asiri's stomach clenched at the word "crazy." It was what everyone had called her before they realized that she actually *could* speak to animals and wasn't just a troubled child seeking attention.

The Amaru regarded her seriously, and then said, *no curse*. Asiri quickly glanced at Dario to see if he had heard the voice too, but he was still scowling at her. So, she was the only one who could hear it, though she could still not understand it as well as she did her animal friends.

Asiri straightened up as tall as she could and met Dario's eyes with her own. "I won't leave it," she said, infusing her voice with as much confidence as she could. "So, either help me, or go. Though, may I remind you that you are an animal healer? This is your job."

Then she turned determinedly on her heel and began wading through the river. After a moment, she heard splashes next to her, and was relieved to see that Dario was following. The truth was, she had no idea what she was going to do when she reached the Amaru and was grateful he had decided to help.

"I thought you didn't even like animals," he said. "And yet here you are, jumping in a river once again to save one of them."

"It's complicated," she answered.

When they reached the other side, they both hesitated, hovering a few feet away from the creature. But when the Amaru let out a pitiful moan, Dario sprang into action.

"Ok buddy, no biting me. No cursing me either, okay?" he said.

Asiri knew that plenty of people spoke to animals without expecting a response, but she was still relieved to see the healer speaking to the creature out loud. It made the "crazy" comment from earlier sting less.

"He's not biting or cursing anyone, isn't that right?" she cooed, sending the Amaru a pointed look. He blinked his llama eyes at her.

No bite, no curse, he said in her head. *Hurts. Help.*

Worried, Asiri inched closer. Dario had approached the Amaru but had yet to touch him, regarding him from a safe distance. She slipped a folding knife from her pocket. "We should get that rope off of him, right?" she asked.

"Where did you get that knife?" he asked, brows high on his forehead.

"How else was I going to cut all the fruit?" she replied.

Kneeling, she handed him the blade, then reached for the Amaru. "Shhh," she said. "We're going to help you."

Her fingers grazed the feathers of the creature's wing, and it was like running her fingers over warm silk. They were impossibly soft to the touch and glistened in the sun like the rippling water beside them. The Amaru stiffened as she came close to the matted mess of flesh and feathers around the rope, but didn't move to pull away or attack them.

"I'll hold his wing, and you cut," she said to Dario.

He shot her an apprehensive glance, but with a deep breath, he nodded. Together, they carefully worked to free the creature from its bindings. It was slow work, almost impossibly slow at times, but together, they moved and shifted like practicing a choreographed dance, instinctively moving to where they were each needed. Twice, Asiri stopped Dario when the Amaru cried out in her mind, waiting until he had calmed once more. Dario never asked her how she knew to stop, but seemed to believe that she was somehow able to perceive the mood and temperament of the animal better than he could. Finally, the last bit of rope fell to the forest floor.

The Amaru attempted to straighten his wing, but then let out an audible yelp. Dario immediately moved to still him.

"In my pack, I have a small mortar and pestle, and there are some green leaves in one of the side pockets," Dario said, and Asiri scrambled to gather it all together. "Put about eight, no, ten leaves in there, and add a little river water. Just a little, to make a paste," he continued, carefully assessing the Amaru's wing. "And there should be a roll of wrapping cloth in there as well."

Asiri scrambled to do what he said, finding all the items in his pack as promised. As she began grinding up the leaves, they released a tacky liquid. Asiri added water little by little until the mixture resembled the paste Dario had requested. She handed it to him.

"Well done," he said, and Asiri felt a rush of pride at his praise. "This looks good. Now we'll need two sturdy sticks, about this long," he motioned with his hands. "I have to set the break, apply the paste, then wrap his wing so he doesn't try to move it for a while."

She hastened to do what he asked, finding the sticks. When she returned, she placed her hand on the Amaru's head, his pain-filled eyes making her heart ache.

"This will hurt, but it will make you better. You must be brave," Dario murmured, and Asiri looked at him, surprised to hear him continue speaking to the creature.

"I'll need your help," Dario continued, looking straight into Asiri's eyes. They were so close that she could see little flecks of amber amongst the honey. Unconsciously, her gaze slid down his face to rest on the beauty mark below his lower lip. Dario swallowed hard and Asiri watched in fascination as his throat moved up and down with the action.

"I mean," he started softly, and she met his gaze again. "Would you help me? Please."

The way he said "please" sent a pleasant hum coursing through her veins. Asiri nodded.

"Of course," she replied, her voice embarrassingly husky. She cleared her throat. "What do you need?"

They stared at one another for a heated moment before a pained sound from the Amaru broke the spell. They both turned their full attention to the creature.

"After I set the break, I'll need you to hold the sticks steady while I apply the salve and wrap the wound," Dario instructed, using his hands to direct her own to the right position. Asiri repressed a shiver at his touch.

When Dario set the break, the Amaru let out a pitiful wail, both externally, and in Asiri's head. She recoiled at the shock of it, but Dario never faltered. He held Asiri's hands firmly in place, and she nodded at him to indicate that she would keep her hold.

Wasting no time, Dario began gently smoothing the paste over the wound. The Amaru trembled, but didn't struggle, and Asiri felt humbled to know he had decided to trust them. Finally, Dario began wrapping the wing with cloth. A warmth blossomed in her chest as she saw the calm, collected way that he handled the creature, and wondered if he was always so attentive and detailed-oriented ...

Especially in bed.

She shook her head to dislodge the thought, feeling the telltale heat of a blush creep over her cheeks. Luckily, Dario's focus centered on helping the Amaru and he didn't notice.

"Well," Dario said. "If he hadn't already cursed me, I'm sure he did now." Asiri noticed that his face was pale, and his forehead beaded with sweat. He truly feared the creature. A deep, generational fear passed down by the people of this land. And yet, despite his unease, he still helped the creature.

Asiri's heart flipped in her chest.

"We can't leave him here," Dario continued. "He's too exposed. And we can't bring him into town. The people would revolt."

Felipe buzzed behind her ear, and Asiri quickly smoothed down her hair, hoping the hummingbird remained well hidden.

"Asiri! There is a small cave nearby. I saw it before I fell in the river. It was empty!" Felipe chirped.

"I think I know of a cave," Asiri told Dario. "Not far from here. We could carry him."

Dario frowned. "I've lived here my entire life. I don't know of any caves nearby."

"There is one! It's just hidden with branches," Felipe insisted.

"I guess you don't know everything," Asiri said lightly. "Come on, we'll lift him together."

Carefully, she and Dario carried the injured Amaru. Asiri followed Felipe's quiet directions, and sure enough, they found a small but serviceable cave not far from the river. It was barely large enough to shelter the large body of the Amaru, but after clearing some branches and vines, they settled the creature inside.

"He'll need more care and time to heal," Dario told her. "He's too big to treat alone. You'll have to help me." He hesitated. "That is, will you? Help me?"

Asiri swallowed down the excitement that sprang up at the prospect of spending more time with Dario. The important thing was making sure the Amaru was all right.

Having an excuse to see Dario more often was just a fortunate side effect.

"I can help," she promised him.

"I have to spend the morning in the clinic," he said. "But I could probably find some time to come out again tomorrow, after midday."

Asiri nodded. "I'll make it work," she promised him.

Together, they stood and began making their way back to Pisqu. Behind them, Asiri heard the faint whisper of the Amaru.

Gracias.

COCK OF THE ROCK/
GALLITO-DE-LAS-ROCAS

CHAPTER 12

DARIO

D ario had just seen an Amaru.

He had just *touched* an Amaru.

Amarus were real.

Dario had always believed in the semidioses, abstractly, in a far-off sort of way. In a "scary children's story" sort of way. In a "sure, they exist but I'll never see one" kind of way.

But now, he had not only seen one, but was treating its injury.

Dario was so distracted by the shock of witnessing a semidios in real life, he almost didn't realize that the woman of his dreams was right there with him the entire time.

Almost.

After all, it was Asiri who had convinced him that they couldn't leave the creature. Though, if he was being honest with himself, he knew that he probably would have ended up trying to help it, anyway; despite his fear of being cursed. But the fact that Asiri had advocated so strongly for the wounded animal made Dario like her even more.

And then, the way that she had sprung into action, leaping back into the river, approaching the Amaru without fear, and following Dario's instructions so well ... he was even more in awe of her.

Dario had come up with a plan. He was going to give Asiri a few days to settle into Pisqu, to get used to the town, and the people, and her new surroundings. Then, he was going to visit the Tienda del Tejido where she worked. He would strike up a conversation, make sure not to talk too much, buy some clothing from her, and then invite her to share a meal with him. He had had it all worked out. But then, he had taken a walk by the river and saw her, motionless and beautiful.

He'd felt elated, thinking it was his chance. But when he moved closer to talk to her, he'd seen the Amaru. All rational thought immediately evaporated from his mind and his plans went out the window.

Luckily for him, by the time he and Asiri had done all that they could for the creature, Dario had come up with a new plan. He convinced Asiri that he wouldn't be able to take care of the Amaru himself, and would need her help. It was a good excuse to see her again, and regularly, at least for the next few days. Thankfully, Asiri had agreed.

He wasn't quite lying to her. While he probably could handle the creature by himself, it would be a lot easier with her help. Besides, the truth was that the Amaru made him feel a bit nervous, and he would feel much more comfortable around it if Asiri was there, too.

Dario still felt dazed when he walked back into his clinic, the waiting area thankfully clear for the moment. Tamya walked out from the back of the practice with Pepe in his sling. The cuy wheeked gently when he saw Dario.

"I'll take him," Dario said automatically, reaching for the guinea pig. Tamya handed him over.

"Are you all right? You look strange," she said with a slight frown.

"Yeah, I'm fine," he lied.

She looked at him more closely, eyes narrowing. Inwardly, Dario sighed. He never was any good at hiding things from his older sister.

Tamya was two years older than him and everything that he was not. She had always been sociable and popular, always at one party or another, and with more friends than Dario could count. She never had any problems dating, and had gone out with several men and women before deciding that "men were a waste of time and women were much more fun." Her face was rounder and more delicate than his, but they shared the same dark eyes and hair, which was currently cut almost as short as his was.

She was his best friend.

"Three animal facts," she said suddenly. "Go!"

Dario smiled. Tamya was the only one who never seemed to want him to be anything but himself. She never told him that he was too loud or too much. She never acted annoyed with him, and beyond their regular sibling fights, they got along with one another better than most people. His sister had the habit of asking him for random facts, or opinions on certain matters, which was basically an invitation to speak as much as he wanted to. It was her reminder to him that he didn't need to change around her.

"All right, three facts!" he agreed. "Number one, an Andean Cock-of-the-Rock gets its name because they are birds that make their nests on rocks, stones, or ledges rather than on tree branch es."[1]

"You already told me that one," Tamya said, faking a large yawn.

"Did I tell you that only the males have bright plumage, while the females have only brown feathers?" he asked her.

"That's number two. And no, you didn't, but I could have guessed that," Tamya said, looking at her nails and pretending to be unimpressed. "Your last one better be pretty good!"

Dario scrunched up his nose. "Fine, number three: females build their nests mostly from mud and different types of plants, and it's bound together by their own saliva."

"Ewww asco!" Tamya shrieked, moving to shove him, but Dario lifted Pepe as a reminder. She settled for punching him lightly on the shoulder while laughing. "All right, that was a good one," she admitted.

Dario smiled back at her, already feeling more relaxed.

"Are you sure there isn't anything else you want to talk about?" she asked, and he hesitated before shaking his head. There was no way he could tell anyone in town—not even his sister—about the Amaru. He didn't want her to worry.

"No, really, I'm fine," he assured her.

"You sure you aren't thinking about a new, dark-haired beauty who works with Doña Iris?" Tamya teased.

Dario's mouth dropped open. "How did you—"

---

1. The Andean cock-of-the-rock is the national bird of Peru. Their feathers often give them the illusion of having a pompadour hairstyle.

Tamya laughed. "It's a small town. People saw you talking to her at Mama Qucha's Cocina. Apparently, you were very close." She waggled her eyebrows at him.

"There's nothing going on there," Dario said quickly.

"But you would like there to be?" she prodded. Dario shot her an exasperated look, but she continued to regard him expectantly.

"But I would like there to be," he finally sighed.

"I knew it!" Tamya screeched, thumping him hard on the back. Dario lurched forward with the force of it, and Pepe let out an indignant squeak at the motion.

"Ya, Tamya!" Dario protested. "Besides, I don't think she likes me much," he admitted ruefully.

"Que? Don't be ridiculous. How could she not like you?" his sister demanded.

Dario shrugged. "You know how I can get, sometimes."

Tamya frowned. "There is nothing wrong with the way that you are."

"But you know I can talk too much," Dario mumbled.

"You are the smartest person that I know!" Tamya insisted. "It's fools who should keep their mouths shut, not you."

"She told me to be quiet," Dario confessed, the memory of it making him duck his head in embarrassment.

"*She did what?*"

Tamya didn't yell. Her voice dropped to a terrifying sort of quiet.

"In her defense, I was talking quite a lot."

"There is no defense!" Tamya bit out. "*How dare she?* Who does she think she is?"

"Tamya, come on, it wasn't her fault!" Dario insisted, his ears growing hot. *Damn,* he thought. *I shouldn't have said anything.* Now Tamya was going to have a bad perception of Asiri, and that was the last thing that he wanted.

"I don't like her," Tamya said, confirming his suspicion.

He sighed. "I do."

He looked back up at his sister sheepishly. Her narrowed eyes relaxed as she took in his expression. Finally, she sighed.

"Fine," she said. "Just make sure she's worth it, Dario."

"I think she is," he started, but she shook her head.

"No, I mean, make sure she likes you for *you*," she told him. "The *real* you. There is nothing wrong with the real you. In fact, he happens to be my favorite person. Make sure you show her that side of you, so you can know if she's worthy of it."

That sounded terrifying to Dario, but he made himself nod.

"Love you, hermanito," Tamya said.

"Love you too, brujita," he answered, and she moved to punch him again.[2] He dodged out of the way with a laugh.

"I'm better now," he promised. "I'm going to go check on the kids in the back."

He and Tamya always called his patients "the kids."

"Well, I'm heading home, but do you need my help tomorrow?" Tamya asked him.

Guilt flitted through his chest. "Do you think you could come around lunchtime? I need to go out and check on a patient."

"Of course," she replied easily.

---

2. "Bruja" means witch. "Brujita" means "little witch." In this case, used as a term of endearment. Kind of.

"Lo siento," Dario said. "I promise I'm trying to find help, I just ..."

"It's fine, hermanito," Tamya insisted. "I don't mind helping out for a while. I know finding the right person is important."

After Tamya left, Dario busied himself with his patients, and worked through a little physical training with poor Pepe. The cuy complained a bit, but Dario was happy to see that he was doing much better.

Then, he sat down and began making a plan for how to treat a semidios.

PYGMY MARMOSET /
TITI PIGMEO

CHAPTER 13

ASIRI

Asiri sat in Paloma's Pastries with her chin resting over her closed fist, watching her friend stir something in a pot. It smelled sweet and delicious, but Asiri was too distracted to fully appreciate it. Her mind was still stuck on the day's earlier events.

She still couldn't believe that she had been in the presence of a semidios. Amarus were not only real, but she could understand them. Not quite like animals, but enough to communicate. The prospect was astounding.

"Paloma," she started carefully. "Why do the people of Pisqu fear Amarus so much?"

Paloma jerked her head towards Asiri, pot in hand forgotten in her shock. Her finger slipped into the hot liquid and she yelped, snatching her hand away from the danger and cradling it to her chest.

"Coño," Paloma muttered.

"I'm so sorry!" Asiri cried out, crossing to her friend. "I didn't mean to distract you!"

Paloma waved her away with her uninjured hand. "Not your fault," she assured her. "It's a caramel burn. I get them all the time." She looked at her left index finger and pouted. Asiri glanced over and sure enough, a blister was already starting to form.

"At least it's not a big one," Paloma said, snapping off a small bit of the sabila plant from a planter by the window, presumably kept for these exact situations.[1] She dabbed some of the cool gel from inside the stalk across her finger in a practiced motion, then quickly pulled the caramel off of the heat.

"Why the curiosity about Amarus?" she asked Asiri, using the hot caramel to shape some swirling candies.

Asiri hesitated. She certainly couldn't tell her friend the truth, but what could she say?

"It's just, all those Amaru deterrents around the river," she answered lamely. "There are so many. They must have taken so much time and labor. It feels like a lot of effort for a creature that might not even exist."

"Oh, Amarus exist!" Paloma said confidently, still shaping candies on the smooth, clean surface in front of her.

Asiri startled but did her best to hide her reaction.

"How can you be so sure?" she asked her.

"Because we are a pueblo by the sea," Paloma explained. "We believe in magia, and miracles, because we see them every day. The ocean is the most wondrous thing in the world. There isn't a sailor alive that doesn't have a story about the calm in a raging tempest, or a miraculous escape from turbulent waves. Every one of them has had a glimpse of a sirena, or a monstro, or even a yacumama

---

1. Aloe vera is better known as sabila in Peru.

hidden beneath its endless depths.[2] There is no fisherman who hasn't felt an eerie stillness over the water, warning them to row home, just in time to escape a life-ending storm, or prayed to Mama Qucha to provide her bounty right before making the catch of their lifetime."

Paloma placed the cooling pot in a sudsy water basin, dusting her hands off on her apron. She looked at Asiri solemnly.

"Magia exists, amiga. That means miraculous beings exist too."

Asiri looked at Paloma in amazement. The way Paloma had spoken so passionately about the ocean made her feel an immense pride to call Pisqu her home. Asiri knew better than most people that magia was real—her gift was proof of that—but hadn't thought about the other ways that magia showed itself in the world.

"But why the fear?" Asiri asked. "Why the deterrents? Amarus are semidioses, which sure, sounds frightening, but why assume that they are evil? If they exist at all?"

"We don't think they're evil," Paloma clarified. "Just terribly bad luck! You're new here, so I don't know if you realize just how superstitious sailors and fishermen can be. There was a story, a long time ago, about an Amaru being spotted right before a great ocean storm that killed many men at sea. Ever since then, they have been a bad omen. To even glimpse one would risk being cursed. In fact, if anyone even thought that they *might* have seen an Amaru, they would have to isolate themselves for a full turn of the moon

---

2. Yacumama means "mother of water" in Quechua.
   Yacumamas are legendary giant serpent beasts, said to devour anything that comes within range.

lest they risk passing that curse on to others. In a pueblo full of oceanfolk, it's just too risky."

Asiri's body flashed hot and cold, and she worried she was going to be sick all over Paloma's clean floors. Had she been reckless? She truly didn't believe that the Amaru was dangerous, and he *had* promised not to curse them. But what did she know of Amarus? Could she truly trust the creature?

Before she could ask any more questions, the front door of Paloma's Pastries flew open, crashing against the wall with a loud bang. Paqari, looking like the reincarnation of Illapa himself, came striding in.[3]

In a flash, Paloma leapt from behind her counter and met him halfway across the shop.

"Qué demonios are you doing here?" she yelled into his face, and Asiri felt taken aback by the anger in her voice.

"Qué demonios am *I* doing here?" He gaped at her. "What in dioses' name do you think *you* are doing here? Do you know what time it is?"

"How did you know I was still here?" Paloma demanded.

"Your lamps are all lit. It's obvious to anyone who walks by that someone is in here," he growled.

"What are you doing on this side of town, anyway?" Paloma demanded. "Shouldn't you be lurking around the docks at this time of night?"

"I was passing by, and I noticed—"" he started, but Paloma interrupted him.

"And noticed *what?*" she demanded.

---

3. Illapa is the Inca warrior god of lightning and thunder.

"That you hadn't gone home yet!" he yelled. "You're still here. What possessed you to stay here all alone this late?"

"Um," Asiri started, trying to draw attention to the fact that Paloma was, in fact, not alone, but Paqari didn't even try to acknowledge her presence.

"Are you really so naive to think that you are safe to walk home alone in the dark at this hour?" he demanded.

Asiri watched as Paloma's face erupted in furious red patches. She shoved against his chest.

"You arrogant, overbearing, condescending, *domineering*—"

"What happened to your finger?" Paqari interrupted her, grabbing the digit which had been punctuating every word with a stiff jab to his sternum. In the commotion, Asiri had forgotten about the burn, and it seemed like Paloma had too.

"What?" Paloma sputtered, her voice still angry. "Oh, I burned it. It's fine." She tried to draw her arm back, but Paqari gripped her wrist tightly with one hand and cradled her injured finger delicately in his other. He ducked his head down for a closer look, then hissed sympathetically when he saw the blister.

"You should be more careful, little bird," he told her, blowing on her finger gently.

Asiri's eyes widened in her face, and her stomach gave a funny little kick. She imagined what it would be like to be in Paloma's position. Except have her hand trapped in Dario's grasp instead, while his mouth ducked closer to her fingers, cool breath blowing against them. Alarmed at the direction of her thoughts, Asiri snapped herself out of the fantasy, surprised to see Paloma and Paqari still a hair's breadth away from one another. Asiri forced out a pointed little cough. Paqari quickly dropped Paloma's hand and stepped away, still not deigning to even look in her direction.

"Take better care of yourself, Palomita," Paqari said before turning around and walking away. "Miguel wouldn't like you taking such risks."

NAUTA
SALAMANDER/
SALAMANDRA

CHAPTER 14

ASIRI

"**A**ll right, I have to ask. Who is Miguel?" Asiri demanded.

After the surprising interaction with Paqari the night before, Paloma had quickly ushered Asiri out of Paloma's Pastries, and scurried home before Asiri could ask her any questions.

Luckily for her, Doña Iris had given her the day off. When Asiri had greeted the woman that morning without a single achiote fruit, and looking worn and tired, the older woman decided that she had been pushing her too hard.

"My fault," she had said. "You just did so well your first few days. I forgot that you had just arrived after traveling a long way. Bodies need rest, you know."

Despite Asiri's protests, the older woman shooed her out of the Tienda del Tejido and told her to "get to know Pisqu." Which suddenly gave Asiri a lot of free time. She wasn't supposed to meet Dario in the woods to care for the Amaru until much later in the day.

Asiri could not wait another second to unravel the mystery of this Miguel person, so she had stolen away to Paloma's Pastries to get some answers.

"Miguel is, well," Paloma shifted, wringing the hem of her apron. "He's mi prometido."

Asiri's mouth dropped open.

"You're *engaged*?" she shrieked.

Paloma sighed. "It's—"

"A long story, yes, yes, you've said. I have time." Asiri said, crossing her arms and looking at Paloma expectantly.

Paloma moved from behind the sweets bar and sat on the stool next to Asiri.

"Bueno," she conceded. "Don't say that I didn't warn you."

Asiri grinned triumphantly.

"Miguel, Paqari, and I grew up together," Paloma started. "We were inseparable. Both my and Miguel's parents worked with Paqari's father on the docks. Our families were partners and very close friends. But when I was eleven, the town found out that Paqari's father was skimming profits from the business, and making illegal trade deals with pirates for more money. It was a shock to us all."

Paloma stopped, a small frown on her face. Asiri just waited, not wanting to interrupt her.

"It was hard for my parents, and for Miguel's, but they eventually recovered," she finally continued. "It was harder for Paqari, whose father left with the pirates when the scandal broke, leaving Paqari alone with his mother and younger brother Ander. His mother became a broken shell of the woman she had once been, withering away in front of all of our eyes. Paqari had refused help from anyone, even my parents, and was determined to care for his family all on his own. He left school, began working on the docks, often the most dangerous and difficult assignments, constantly putting himself at risk."

Her voice cracked, but she didn't cry. "After that, he didn't want to spend time with me and Miguel anymore," Paloma confessed softly. "He was too busy working, making sure his family was all right. He got a bit of a reputation around the town as a bad boy, but I don't know if he was actually doing bad things or if he was just guilty by association with his father. Anyway, he didn't want me and Miguel in his life anymore. So Miguel and I got close."

She smiled at Asiri. "You know, there was a time where I thought I would end up with Paqari. I had the *biggest* crush on him growing up."

Had? Asiri thought to herself. *Are you sure about that past tense?* Paloma's reaction to Paqari's late-night visit did not seem like the actions of a woman who was unaffected. But Asiri was smart enough not to voice her skepticism out loud.

"But when he stopped coming around, Miguel and I connected in our loneliness. We both missed him. And eventually, we fell in love," Paloma continued.

"We were seventeen when he proposed. The entire town threw a huge party, completely over the top. They all loved us, felt like they had a claim on us, in a way. Everyone had watched us grow up together, then they watched us fall in love. They waited for us to figure out our feelings, and confess to each other how we felt. They rejoiced. The town's golden boy and girl, together at last. The day he asked me to be his wife felt so perfect, so right. Like nothing could ever come between us."

A storm gathered behind the dark brown of Paloma's eyes, and Asiri instinctively reached over to cover her friend's hand. Paloma squeezed it gratefully.

"Then he told me that he was joining the crew of a merchant ship. You see, after Paqari's father, his family never fully recovered financially from their loss. Miguel said he didn't want to marry me as a poor man. He said that I deserved better. I begged him not to go. I told him that I didn't care, that we would make our own way together, but he wouldn't listen.

'One year,' he promised me. 'One year, just to get us started. I'll be back next summer and make you my wife.'"

"Wow," Asiri murmured, too stunned to know what else to say. "So, your childhood sweetheart is off to sea, and you are here waiting."

"Please don't say it's romantic," Paloma pleaded, shutting her eyes tight.

"Actually, I was going to say that it sounds awful. And incredibly unfair to you. You didn't even get a say? That's bullshit."

Paloma's eyes flew open, and she stared at Asiri with what looked like utter shock.

"Yes," she finally breathed, stretching out the word. She clutched Asiri's hand tighter. "Yes, it was *bullshit*."

"But you can't tell anyone in town that," Asiri said, beginning to understand. "Because they all think it's sweet. They think it's beautiful, the daring groom, off to secure his fortune for his patient bride."

Paloma nodded vigorously.

"And I *was* patient! Oh amiga, the first two years I did nothing but wait patiently. I was the dutiful novia, waiting for her man to return from the sea. For two years I waited, my lungs filled with salt air and my heart floating on the ocean's waves. In the third year I worried instead. I lived in a state of constant anxiety and fear. I was a lighthouse without a beacon, spinning aimlessly. It was terrible. It was the worst thing that I had ever experienced."

Paloma sprang up from her chair and began pacing the room.

"In year four, I accepted that Miguel had either died, or decided not to return to me. That year was even worse. I'm ashamed to admit that some days I wasn't even sure which option broke my heart more.

By the fifth year, the tides began to shift. I started getting over him."

She turned to look at Asiri.

"It's been *seven years,* Asiri. Seven years! I grew up. I left home. I buried my father and took care of my mother. I built up Palomas Pastries from scratch, made it into a successful business. But no matter what I do, no matter how old I get, no matter how many years pass, everyone in this town still sees me as Miguel's girl. Not as a young woman, not as a business owner, not even as just Paloma. *Miguel's girl.* And I'm *exhausted.* You're the only one I can tell this to; since you didn't know Miguel, you didn't see us grow up together. You didn't watch us fall in love with each other. But that was such a long time ago. Don't I deserve a life outside of Miguel?"

"Of course you do, amiga," Asiri assured her, then stood up to gather her in for a hug. She couldn't begin to imagine what it was like for Paloma, but she did know a little of how it felt to live a sort of half-life, always underneath someone else's shadow.

"You deserve your own life," she repeated, both to Paloma and to herself.

Paloma pulled back and dabbed her eyes with a napkin pulled from her apron pocket. "These are happy tears," she assured Asiri. "I'm just so grateful to have a friend like you. There is no one else I can tell these things to. And it's so nice to finally have someone to share secrets with."

Paloma beamed at her, and Asiri felt guilt churn in her gut. Her new friend was being open and honest with her, and she was repaying her by keeping secrets.

"Wait," Paloma said, cocking her head and regarding her seriously. "You have a secret too, don't you?!" She clapped her hands with excitement. "You don't have to tell me, of course," she quickly added. "But I do hope you know that you can."

"I—" Asiri started, then stopped, biting her lip.

Could I tell her? Asiri wondered. *About my gift? About my life at the Casa de Murmuros? About the Amaru?*

But even as she thought it, she knew it wasn't possible. Dario loved animals, and even he had been willing to walk away from the Amaru out of fear. How could she expect Paloma, who had grown up in a town full of terror and superstition towards the creature, to understand?

Of course, Dario had changed his mind, hadn't he? He had fought through his fear in order to help the Amaru. The handsome man was brilliant with the creature too, patient and kind. He had taken charge right away and did everything in his power to help and heal the Amaru. A rush of warmth flooded Asiri at the memory of his steady hands and gentle movements.

"I bet I can guess your secret, though," Paloma said cheekily. "Does it have something to do with a certain animal healer?"

Asiri gasped. How much did Paloma know?

"I knew it!" Paloma cried out. "You like him, don't you! Don't deny it, you should see how much you're blushing right now!"

Asiri *was* blushing, she could feel the warmth in her cheeks and neck. "I suppose he is rather handsome," she admitted.

"Handsome? He's downright dreamy! Not my type, of course, but I have eyes, don't I? And he's a great guy. You could do a lot worse!" Paloma said.

"Nothing can happen there," Asiri insisted.

"Why not? You're both adults. You're both single. What's the problem?" Paloma asked.

"I—It's just—I couldn't, ok? Trust me." Asiri insisted.

Paloma just grinned impishly. "We'll see," she said.

"We'll see."

Despite her insistence to Paloma that nothing could happen between herself and Dario, Asiri couldn't help but feel nervous on her way to meet him and the Amaru.

"Why can't anything happen between you and the healer?" Felipe asked her, flying in front of her instead of perching on her shoulder. "I like him."

"I like him too," Asiri admitted. "But I can't. I came here to be different. To live a different life. If people start learning about my gift, then they might start to want me to use it for them. I don't want to live for anyone else again. I want to live for me."

Following Felipe's directions, Asiri finally made it back to the cave and realized that Dario had already beaten her there. She could see him kneeling in the dirt, muttering to himself.

"Hola," she called out softly, not wanting to startle him or the Amaru. He turned and flashed her a sweet smile that made her lower belly clench.

"Hola," he greeted her. Glancing back toward the Amaru, his smile slipped. "I'm trying to get him to eat, but he won't."

He ran an aggravated hand through his hair, and some fell over his forehead. Asiri resisted the urge to push it off his face. Asiri kneeled next to him and focused on the Amaru. He looked the same as yesterday, although his eyes appeared more sullen than pained today.

"Hi again," she said softly, and the Amaru shifted.

No grass, he said in her head.

No grass? Asiri wondered, frowning. She looked over at Dario and saw that he held a fistful of grass in his hands.

"You were feeding him grass?" she asked him.

Dario let out an exasperated breath. "I was trying. The stubborn thing won't eat."

No grass, the Amaru repeated.

"Maybe it doesn't eat grass?" she suggested.

"Maybe it doesn't eat at all. We don't even know if semidioses need to eat." He sat back on his heels. "But if it *does* eat, we need to figure out what right away. It's not just about hunger, though that is important, of course. But it is also important that he continues to receive the vitamins and minerals that animals need to consume for their proper care. Did you know that immune systems—that is, the thing inside of us that helps to fight against infections—rely on proper nutrition for optimal function?"

Dario took a deep breath and opened his mouth as if to continue, but then caught Asiri staring at him. He fascinated her. How did he know so much about all of this? It was obvious that he was passionate about the information, too. When he was speaking, his voice became higher, and his speech faster, almost tripping over his words in his excitement. She hoped he would continue, but instead, he snapped his jaw shut and took a deep breath from his nose.

"Sorry," he mumbled, and Asiri cocked her head, confused as to what he was apologizing for. Before she could ask, he continued.

"I am doing my best to treat him like he's one of my other patients," he said in an even voice. "And that includes building their strength back up, but I may be out of my depth here."

No grass, the Amaru said yet again.

"Ok, stop!" Asiri muttered.

"I am just voicing my frustration at not knowing how to help him!" Dario snapped, physically distancing himself from her.

Asiri could have kicked herself. *You're doing it again!* she thought, exasperated.

"No, I mean, stop being so hard on yourself," she amended quickly, and he visibly relaxed. "I'm sure we can find the solution. First things first: why grass?"

"He is a llama. I mean, he has the head of a llama, right? So wouldn't he eat grass?" Dario's voice was uncertain. Asiri was just as lost as he was.

"What do you eat?" Asiri asked the Amaru, hoping Dario wouldn't think she was actually expecting a response, even though she very much was.

Fish, the Amaru said in her mind. *Fish, fish, fish.*

Well, that was helpful.

"What if we tried fish?" she asked Dario, who looked at her oddly.

"Why fish?" he asked her, more curious than accusatory.

"Well," Asiri scrambled for a plausible reason. "He is a river god, right? So he must live beneath the river. Maybe he eats what the river provides, too?"

Fish, fish, fish, the Amaru insisted. Asiri clenched her jaw, but ignored him.

"It's a good idea," Dario said, looking thoughtful. "I wish I had thought of it. It's worth a try, right?"

Removing a piece of string from his pack, Dario crossed to the river, and Asiri sent a quick prayer up to the dioses that he would catch something. She needn't have worried. After only a few moments, he returned with a shiny, fat fish. When he brought it close to the Amaru, the creature gobbled it up whole.

Fish, fish! It insisted, bouncing a little.

"Looks like he's still hungry," Dario said, looking pleased. "That's a good sign. Try to make him stop moving so much, I don't want him to jostle his wing. I will catch a few more fish."

Fish! Fish! the Amaru demanded.

"Yes, he's getting more fish. Now sit still so you don't hurt yourself," Asiri whispered to him, and to her surprise, he stopped bouncing right away. Instead, he leaned his large llama head against her chest and let out a contented sigh. Deeply moved by the action, tears sprung to Asiri's eyes.

Fish, he repeated happily.

"Yes baby," Asiri squeezed through the tightness in her throat. "He's bringing you more fish."

SECHURAN FOX/ ZORRO SECO

CHAPTER 15

ASIRI

Once the Amaru ate his fill, it was time for Asiri and Dario to apply more salve and re-wrap his injured wing. If they had thought that the process would be as seamless as it had been the day prior, they were sorely mistaken.

"Oof, ouch, hold still," Asiri grumbled as the Amaru shifted, butting his head hard into her shoulder. Beads of sweat were visible on Dario's forehead as he tried to wrangle the creature's wriggling body. Together, the two of them removed the gauze, but the Amaru was not allowing them to get close enough to treat and re-bandage his wound.

"Will you hold still? We are trying to help you," Asiri tried telling him, but the Amaru only struggled harder.

Hurts. Stings.

"I know it hurts!" Asiri answered. "But you won't get better unless you let us help!"

"Well, he certainly got some of his strength back," Dario grunted as the Amaru whipped its tail around and slapped him on the back of the head. "Maybe next time we save the fish for after the treatment."

"Maybe next time we won't give him fish at all," Asiri threatened, trying her best to hold the Amaru's wing steady. Narrowing his eyes at her, the Amaru growled.

Fish! he yelled in her head.

"If you keep acting like a brat then—"

FISH, the Amaru roared, and lightning cracked hard and fast across the sky.

"What the," Dario started, when suddenly his eyes grew into twin moons on his face. "Asiri, look out!"

Asiri spun just in time to see the water from the river shoot up into an angry torrent in the sky. It hung there like a sourceless waterfall until suddenly exploding outward in a fury. Droplets splashed all over herself and Dario, leaving their clothing drenched. Asiri sputtered and looked back at the Amaru. She could swear the little beast was looking proud of himself.

Dario met her eyes warily. "Do we think he did that?" he asked her.

"Well, he is a river god. I guess he can control the water?" she guessed.

They looked at the Amaru, who was suddenly much more calm. His llama mouth opened into a large, teeth-baring yawn, and he shifted his head onto Asiri's lap, promptly falling asleep.

Asiri and Dario shared a quick look of incredulity before springing to work. Whatever he had done must have tired him out, because he stayed asleep as they treated his injury and wrapped up his wing once more.

Once she and Dario were done, Asiri lifted his heavy head as gingerly as she could, and placed it on a soft pile of leaves. They stood slowly, not wanting to disturb him, and began walking away quietly. Finding the river, which was flowing as normally as it ever was, they began following it back to Pisqu.

The day was warm and their clothes dried rapidly as they walked. A gentle breeze flirted through the trees often enough to provide a respite from the heat. Asiri noticed a few frogs and salamanders sunning themselves on the jutting rocks framing the river's path, while birds danced and preened on the thick trunks of tree branches.

Dario was wearing a cream tunic with a border of fawn-colored chakanas at its hem. The fabric was taut against his broad shoulders and chest, the river water and the humidity making it cling to areas that Asiri found it hard to glance away from. She did her best to keep her gaze towards the ground and away from the expanse of his muscles and flesh, and blamed her burning cheeks and shortness of breath on the heat.

Asiri and Dario walked quietly for quite some time, and even when they were far enough away that the Amaru would not hear them, they still kept their silence.

Asiri chewed on her lower lip.

"Say something to him, Asiri!" Felipe encouraged behind her ear, and she winced at both the sound and the advice.

"Are you all right?" Dario asked, and Asiri quickly nodded.

"Yes, yes, fine," she said, her voice sounding too high.

He held her gaze for a long moment, then opened his mouth as if to say something. Asiri held her breath, but he simply shook his head and kept walking instead.

"Que?" she asked him.

"Nada," he answered.

They walked silently for a few more steps, curiosity burning in Asiri's chest. Scraping up all her courage, she tried again. "You looked like you wanted to say something," she commented.

He looked at her, then away. Then at her again, his lips drawn into a thin line.

"You say you don't like animals," he finally said. "But you have gone out of your way to help them. You interact with the Amaru without hesitation. You even pet him, and let him fall asleep on your lap. When the water, when the river ..." He ran his hand over the stubble that was just visible over his jaw. "You didn't even seem scared. You didn't treat him any differently afterward. It just doesn't seem like the actions of someone who dislikes animals."

Instinctively, Asiri's left hand came up to her shoulder, grazing the hair that hid Felipe from view.

"It's not—" she hesitated. "It's not that I don't like animals."

Dario didn't seem surprised. He simply nodded.

"I simply can't work with them," she confessed. She couldn't elaborate. She couldn't tell him the truth. But she didn't want to lie to him either. Not any more than she had to.

After a few moments, Dario nodded again. "It isn't easy, seeing them injured or in pain. Knowing sometimes you don't know what to do or how to help, or that even if you do everything right, it still might not be enough. I can understand that."

It wasn't the real reason, but it was a very good reason. Asiri had only ever thought about how wonderful it would be to have the medical knowledge to help the injured animals she came across. She never imagined what it would be like to have that knowledge and still not be able to save them.

"That sounds very difficult," she said softly.

Dario stopped walking and turned to look at her straight on. "It can be," he confessed. "Sometimes I wish I could talk to the animals, actually understand what ails them."

Asiri nearly choked on her own heart. It felt like it flew straight up into her throat. She tensed, her shoulders drawing up sharply toward her ears, making Felipe chirp in protest.

Does he know? she thought. *Is he testing me?* Her hand reached up and clutched at her mother's necklace for reassurance.

But Dario didn't sound accusatory. He didn't look at her curiously, or wait to see how she would respond to the fact that he wished he could speak to animals. He simply continued.

"If they could tell me their symptoms, like human patients can to doctors, it would be so much easier." He sighed. "But I would rather try, and risk being hurt, than not try, and keep my feelings safe. This way, at least I feel like I am making some sort of difference."

Asiri felt herself relax. He wasn't trying to trap her. He was simply a kind man who truly cared for his patients. She smiled at him, a true smile, unguarded and warm. He blinked at her.

"You *are* making a difference," she told him earnestly, and the tips of Dario's ears turned pink.

"You are too," he told her.

Asiri's eyes went wide. "Me? I haven't done anything!" she protested.

"You have," Dario responded. "You saved the colibrí. You are helping the Amaru, even though he is supposed to be a creature of ill-omen. You have made a difference to them."

Asiri felt Felipe kiss her skin with his beak in agreement, but still she shook her head. "It doesn't feel like enough," she admitted.

Dario's hand lifted, gently cupping her cheek. His skin was warm and smooth.

"It never does," he said softly. "But I like that you try."

The heart that had leapt into Asiri's throat just moments before now thundered throughout every inch of her body. She could feel the fast, rhythmical beats in her stomach, behind her breasts, in the tips of her fingers, but mostly on her lips. They suddenly felt very full and heavy, parting on their own. Dario's thumb swept softly, almost imperceptibly, down towards her mouth and Asiri's breath hitched. Dario shifted, leaning towards her, and the air became charged with energy, like the fuzzy electric sparks she sometimes felt when handling the fabrics in the Tienda del Tejidos. Dario was so close to her now, his eyes dark and intent. Asiri allowed her own to flutter shut.

"If you carry on the way you are, I will vomit in this cage!" a loud, crotchety voice yelled out, snapping her out of her trance.

Asiri jolted, springing back from Dario. For a moment he stood frozen, hand still suspended in the air, his upper body leaning forward.

He looked delicious, all bronze muscles and full lips, gazing at her like he wanted nothing more than to have her in his arms. Asiri had an overwhelming urge to step back into his space, pick up where they had left off and see where the moment took them, when the voice screeched again.

"Sure! Sure, forget old Marco here! Leave me to die! Leave me to starve! Leave me to perish from thirst in this heat!"

Asiri looked around, trying to find the angry cuy, but could not see him. Dario dropped his hand quickly and stepped back from her, furrowing his brows.

"I apologize, I—" he started, when Marco interrupted.

"Apologizing to her? Why apologize to her? It's me that you left to catch my death in the rain!"

Asiri looked up; it was nowhere close to raining.

"Any manner of predators could have come and made a meal of poor old Marco!" the guinea pig yelled, apoplectic.

"Do you hear that?" Asiri interrupted Dario. Marco's outraged cries drown out Dario's words before they could leave his lips.

Dario stopped and listened, his face still drawn up in confusion.

"I will stuff kernels of corn in your nostrils while you sleep, and you will grow stalks out of your nose! I will pluck each individual hair from your legs! I will invite every rodent in your neighborhood to fornicate on your bedsheets!"

Asiri winced, but Dario nodded.

"Oh, of course," he said, striding over to a cluster of trees. "I didn't want to leave Pepe alone in the clinic, but I also didn't want to startle him by bringing him too close to the Amaru," he explained while hauling a sturdy-looking cage from between the trunks.

"My name is not Pepe!" the guinea pig raged. "It is Marco Ignacio Lorenzo Gonzales Palacios—"

"I'm surprised you could hear his squeaking!" Dario continued.

"I will send my ancestors to haunt your nightmares!" Marco continued. "I will shred every single one of your pillows and strew their feathers on every surface you own!"

"Just barely," Asiri lied.

Dario removed Pepe—*Marco*—from the cage and put him back in the same sling Asiri had seen him in the day that they had met. Then Dario turned back to face her awkwardly.

"Well," he said. "I should ..." he trailed off, motioning in a direction.

Asiri nodded, disappointed. "Of course. And I should—" she motioned in the opposite direction. "I still have ingredients to find for Doña Iris."

It was a lie. It was her day off. She just didn't trust herself to remain in his presence while Marco shouted obscenities at her.

"Of course," Dario responded, but made no move to leave. He shifted from one foot to the other, then cleared his throat.

"Mañana?" he asked tentatively. "Around the same time? To take care of the Amaru, that is."

Asiri shot him a shy smile and nod. "Of course."

His shoulders relaxed, and he edged his way towards her. "You really were great with him today," he murmured. His voice dropped, low and husky, and Asiri's toes curled in her shoes.

"We make a good team." She hadn't meant to whisper, but her voice was barely audible over the babbling stream.

Dario leaned in again, and Asiri held her breath. His face was a breath away from hers -

when Marco shat all over Dario's tunic.

CHINCHILLA/
CHINCHILLA

CHAPTER 16

DARIO

D ario could have killed Pepe.

"You're lucky that you're adorable," he told him as he scrubbed his tunic with the strongest soap he owned. "Because that stunt you just pulled has me seriously considering breaking your other two legs."

Pepe began purring, and Dario melted.

"Just kidding, bud," he said. "I know it wasn't your fault. You didn't mean to."[1]

Once he and the guinea pig were clean and comfortable again, Dario finally let himself think about his moment with Asiri.

Did we almost kiss? he wondered. *Did she want to kiss?*

Dario couldn't be sure. They had such a good day, working together and laughing at the Amaru's antics. Even the semidios hadn't seemed as imposing as before, not with Asiri there by his side. He had seemed like any regular animal, wounded and in need of help. The more time he spent in Asiri's presence, the more he grew to like her.

---

1. Marco absolutely DID "mean to."

She was clearly smart. Not simply in the well-educated sort of way, which was apparent by the way that she spoke and carried herself. That sort of smart never impressed Dario much, anyway. He never did very well in school because it was hard for him to pay attention to the lessons that didn't interest him. Once he could focus on animal healing, he realized that there were different types of intelligences, and just because he hadn't done well at school didn't mean that he couldn't do well in life.

But Asiri was different kinds of smart too. She was so good with animals, the way that she held them and spoke to them and soothed them was instinctual. She had figured out what the Amaru ate, which was a relief for Dario. And he had heard around town that she was becoming invaluable to Doña Iris and the Tienda del Tejido. If he couldn't have her by his side helping him with his patients, he was glad that at least the older woman had the pleasure of Asiri's company.

She was also brave. Twice now, she had flung herself into the river to help an animal; she had approached the Amaru without fear. When the river had jumped up and exploded outward, raining water all over them, she had barely flinched. Even then, he was fairly certain it was from the shock of the water, rather than from fear.

But with Asiri, it felt like one step forward, two steps back. Just when he thought that they were getting closer, she would retreat from him.

Maybe I'm just seeing what I want to see, Dario thought. It wasn't like she was sending clear signals, if anything, the woman blew hot and cold daily. *I shouldn't assume that. Just because I feel inexorably drawn to her doesn't mean that she feels the same way.*

His sister's words echoed in his mind. "Make sure you show her the real you, so you can know if she's worthy of it." If she only liked him some of the time, that wasn't good enough for him. As much as he wanted it to be. Tamya was right. He deserved someone who didn't find him overwhelming. Who didn't think he was "too much."

By the time he returned to his clinic, Dario was feeling more dejected than he had since his breakup with his ex. Sullenly, he managed to place Pepe back in his cage before Tamya burst in, frantic.

"What are you doing? Why aren't you ready?" she demanded.

"Ready?" he repeated with a frown.

Tamya's face fell. "Oh Dario, you forgot again, didn't you?"

Dario blinked at her, his mind shuffling through all the important things that he was supposed to remember. Tasks and chores flashed behind his eyes, like rifling through stacks of papers until he snagged on one.

Damn.

"We're seeing mamá y papá today," he said, closing his eyes in resignation. Dario loved his parents, he really did, but visiting with them wasn't always fun. They had a way of always making him feel like he was still that over-excitable little boy, not the professional, adult man that he had become.

"I did remind you," Tamya said softly. He knew she wasn't saying it to make him feel bad, but it made his shoulders slump, anyway. Even with Tamya's helpful nudges, he had a habit of forgetting things. Dario always tried to remember, he would write things down and leave himself notes, but more often than not those notes would end up forgotten as well.

"They wanted me to bring a new birdhouse," he said, rushing out the door to the clinic's small backyard. When they had asked him a month ago, Dario had started working on it right away. Now he pulled back a thick tarp to reveal the bare bones of a half-completed project collecting dust, and his heart sank.

"I can do it," he told Tamya, who sighed.

"I'll go get you some fresh clothes from your house, and you can wash up in the clinic baths when you're finished. But if you're not done in an hour, I'm leaving without you."

Dario felt a rush of gratitude and he tried to give Tamya a hug, but she wriggled away from him, wrinkling her nose. "Why do you smell like shitrus?"

A little over an hour later, Dario was clean, wearing new clothes, and holding a completed birdhouse under his arm.

"I still don't know how you finished that so quickly," Tamya said as they walked up the stairs to their parent's home.

"You know me, always better under pressure," he replied, which was true. He often wished that he could manage his time better, but most of his responsibilities ended up being pushed aside until there was a sudden, looming deadline. Dario took a deep breath and gave a quick knock on the door before stepping inside.

"We're here!" Tamya called out, crossing to where their father was standing from his favorite chair. He gave her a big hug, then placed a hand on her closely cropped hair.

"Did you cut this again?" he said with a frown.

"Hello to you," was Tamya's only reply. Their mother appeared from the kitchen, her brightly embroidered apron over a deep red shirt that matched the paint on her lips.

"You're late," she told them both with a frown, but accepted a kiss from Tamya and a one-armed hug from Dario. "Te olvidaste?"

Dario was about to admit his mistake and begin groveling when Tamya interrupted.

"Nope, we were on our way out when someone had a pet emergency. Luckily, the chinchilla will pull through, thanks to Dario."

He shot her a grateful smile as his mother sniffed and turned back to the kitchen. "You owe me one," his sister mouthed at him behind their mother's back.

"Well, go set the table so we can eat. Your father must be starving," Mama said.

Dario turned to his dad and handed him the birdhouse.

"Couldn't paint it?" Papa said while examining it with a shrug. An itchy, uncomfortable feeling unfurled in Dario's stomach. "Well, I suppose that's okay," his father continued. "Gracias."

Tamya and Dario set the table as their mother placed dish after dish of food on the sturdy wooden surface. First was a large clay bowl filled with ceviche de pescado, the delicate chunks of white fish cooked in lime juice and flavored with aji amarillo. She stacked large oval slices of bright orange camote on a plate along with fat kernels of choclo to counteract the acidity. An entire pollo a la brasa sat in the center of the table, marinated with garlic, herbs, and spices, and roasted on a spit until the skin was brown and crispy. Slices of potato surrounded it, soaking in its juice.

At first, they were quiet, only the sounds of chewing and groans of delight filling the room. Then their parents began their usual round of chismes.

"Tu tio Alfonso broke his foot last week chasing after a loose hen,"

"You know Susanna, from your school? Well, her son just caught the largest fish their village has ever seen!"

"Jaime, the neighbor two doors down? He got a new dog that will not stop barking at night!"

"Tu prima Priscilla se va casar," Mama said slyly, looking at Tamya.

His sister ignored the pointed stare and took another big bite of pollo. "That's nice. She's always wanted to get married," she replied with a full mouth.

"She is five years younger than you, and already getting married! When are you going to find a nice man to settle down with?" Mama asked.

Dario saw Tamya's jaw tense.

"Or woman," he added. His mother looked at him with furrowed brows.

"Que?" she asked.

"When will she find a nice man *or woman* to settle down with," he repeated, and caught Tamya's eye; they shared a smile.

"Si, si, fine, man or woman," his mother amended.

"Why are you asking me? Why aren't you asking Dario? He's the one with a new girlfriend," Tamya said, and all the close familial warmth he had been feeling towards his sister evaporated on the spot.

"Que?" his mother shrieked, while his father clapped him on the back.

"No, what? No, I don't!" Dario sputtered, lime dribbling down his chin. He glared at his two-faced sister.

"Well, if she isn't your girlfriend yet, what are you waiting for? You are obviously interested in her," she answered.

"No, I'm not, why would you ..." he trailed off at her triumphant expression. "I mean ... who?" he finished lamely.

"Please," she scoffed.

"Tell us about her, hijo!" his mother beamed at him. "Who is she? What is her name? What is she like?"

Dario looked around at three pairs of eyes staring at him expectantly, and with a groan, dropped his head into his hands.

Hours later, Dario walked home, feeling beaten and bruised. His mamá y papá were good people, and he knew that they loved him and Tamya very much. But no matter how old he got, visiting them always made him feel like a little kid again. He found himself striving to gain their approval, telling them about his practice and his patients and his life, which always resulted in him talking too fast and for too long. Which in turn only served to exasperate his parents, who had to remind him to settle down.

For a while, he managed to deflect their line of questioning regarding Asiri, but was less successful at diverting her from his thoughts. He came to a decision. As difficult as it would be, he concluded that it was too difficult to be around Asiri. Being near her, but consistently feeling like he was messing things up, or doing something wrong, was simply too difficult. He had worked really hard to grow into the man that he had become, and he was proud of the person that he was. Being around her made him doubt himself, and he didn't like it.

Seeing his parents only reinforced his decision. Though they might not have intended to, they always managed to make him feel inadequate, and he knew that he deserved better than that. He would no longer accept it; from anyone. So, as Dario approached the village, he continued walking right past the road that would lead him to his home, and instead began walking towards the Tienda del Tejido. He felt his heart sink with every step he took.

When he arrived at the store, he took a moment to steal his nerves. He would tell Asiri that he no longer needed help tending to the Amaru, and that there was no reason to keep meeting in the forest. It would be hard. He had gotten used to the idea of seeing her daily, but it was for the best. Gathering every last scrap of his courage, he quietly slipped inside. Dario recognized Asiri's long hair immediately, her profile to him as she assisted another customer. He quickly stood behind a long hanging cloth, deciding to wait until she finished. Then he heard a voice that made his blood run cold.

"No, this isn't what I'm looking for either," the feminine voice said primly. "Listen, I know that you're new here, so why don't you get Doña Iris? No offense, honey, she'll just be able to help me better."

Dario's skin prickled at her dismissive tone towards Asiri, but he leaned back further into the shadows, not wanting to be spotted.

"Of course," Asiri answered her cheerily, and he could hear her soft footsteps heading towards the back of the store.

Then he was alone with the last person in the world he wanted to be alone with. Dario breathed as shallowly as he could, praying to any dios that would listen that she would not wander to the front of the store that concealed him. To his horror, he heard soft rustles moving through the piles of fabrics and aisles of clothing heading his way. He heard a soft humming and saw a shadow cutting closer and closer to his hiding spot. Dario's shoulders tensed as he prepared for his inevitable discovery, when suddenly Doña Iris's voice cut through the tienda.

"Belinda!" the older woman greeted her. Gratitude washed over Dario as he saw the shadow recede back towards the center of the store. He allowed himself a quiet sigh of relief.

"Doña Iris," Belinda greeted her. "Como estas?"

"Bien, bien, niña, gracias," Iris replied. "Y tu? And where is that fine gentleman of yours today?"

Dario startled and peeked through a gap in the hanging fabric just in time to watch Belinda wrinkle her nose.

"Do you mean Dario?" she asked with a delicate sniff. "I ended that ages ago. I mean, sure, he's very handsome, but *dioses*, that man never shuts up."

Shame erupted in Dario's chest at her words, radiating heat through his limbs. His shoulders slumped. He didn't dare look at where Asiri was standing. He was afraid that at any second she would agree with her.

Please let Belinda leave it at that, he thought. *Don't say anything more in front of Asiri!*

"I mean, at first it was fine, but after a while it was all 'did you know this?' and 'the lifecycle of a butterfly' that. I swear that man would bring a caiman to his home if he could, just to better study it, and then talk for hours about its diet. The man is exhausting."

Dario felt like he might be sick.

"I think that would be fascinating," he heard. Peeking through the cloth again, it shocked him to see that it was Asiri who had spoken, her arms crossed rigidly over her chest.

"Que?" Belinda asked, looking at Asiri derisively.

"How many people could tell you about proper vicuña hoof care, or the native habitats of marmosets, or the shedding cycles of emerald tree boas?" Asiri continued. Dario felt his mouth part in surprise.

"Why would anyone care about any of that?" Belinda demanded.

Asiri simply shrugged. "I care. I think it's amazing what Dario does and how much he knows about the world. He's incredibly smart."

Dario felt his heart kick in his chest. He could count on one hand how many times he had been called "smart" in his life.

"Besides, there is nothing more attractive than someone who is passionate. It doesn't matter what they are passionate about, just seeing the light and excitement in their eyes when they feel comfortable sharing something that they care about with you is a gift." Asiri continued. "I have been lucky enough to hear him talk like that a few times now, and I am always impressed."

Her recusal of Belina shocked Dario. He had been under the impression that he had been annoying her. Had he been mistaken?

Dario watched as Belinda narrowed her eyes at Asiri. "*Passion* was never the problem between me and Dario," she said, sickly sweet. A pretty pink flush crept over Asiri's cheeks. Belinda then turned pointedly towards Doña Iris.

"I am here to see if you have anything new. My family and I are traveling to Ica to visit relatives, and I want to make sure I am the best dressed of all my primas."

"Of course," Doña Iris murmured. "Why don't you come to the back to check? Asiri, why don't you go grab us some cafecitos from el cafetero down the street?"

Then she and Belinda walked towards the back of the store, chatting amongst themselves. Dario watched as Asiri took a deep breath, smoothing her hands down her dark tunic. Then, with a sigh, she walked purposefully towards the front door.

Dario stepped out of his hiding spot a moment too late, watching as she disappeared down the street. Frowning, he could have sworn that he saw a hummingbird dash from some bushes to perch on her shoulder. Shaking his head, he began making his way home, Asiri's words echoing in his head the entire way back.

Maybe there was hope after all.

ALPACA /
ALLPAQA

CHAPTER 17

ASIRI

"I think Dario almost kissed me," Asiri said the next morning, plopping down on what was fast becoming "her stool" in Paloma's Pastries.

Paloma squealed, throwing her hands up in the air and flinging flour absolutely everywhere.

"I knew it!" she shrieked, bouncing on her heels. "Didn't I say so?"

Just then, a well put-together looking gentleman entered the shop, making his way towards the counter. Without missing a beat, Paloma sliced off a fat slice of tres leches cake, plopped it onto a plate, then shoved the entire thing in the man's hands along with a fork.

"Here you go, on the house. You can return the plate tomorrow," she said, shuffling him back outside. The bewildered man didn't even have a second to protest before Paloma slammed the door in his face, locking it after him. Striding back to an open-mouthed Asiri, Paloma grinned. "He's going to love that cake," she said, jerking her thumb backwards towards the store entrance.

"Now," she continued, settling into the seat beside Asiri. "Tell me *everything*!"

"Paloma!" Asiri laughed, scandalized. "You shouldn't have done that! There's nothing to tell, truly!"

"You said you kissed! That is definitely something. Now talk!" Paloma answered, pointing a flour-dusted finger in Asiri's face.

"I said *almost*. *Almost* kissed. And I said I *think* we almost kissed. I mean, I'm pretty sure we did ..." doubt crept up Asiri's spine, then spun around and settled in her stomach. They had, hadn't they? It certainly felt like they were about to kiss. Was she reading too much into things?

Paloma motioned wildly for her to continue. Quickly, Asiri went over the events of the day before, not mentioning the part about the Amaru, of course. She explained that she met Dario out while she was collecting materials and that they had talked and gotten close. Then, the almost kiss, and the ill-timed bowel movement of a certain grumpy guinea pig.

Paloma laughed so hard she could barely catch her breath. Asiri couldn't help but join her.

"Oh Asiri, what *shit timing*," Paloma cackled.

"Yeah, it really *stunk*." Asiri added through her giggles.

"I guess between you and the cuy, you were priority *number two?*" Paloma was nearly bent over with laughter.

"Well, after that, Dario went home. As an animal healer, it was his *doody*."

Both Asiri and Paloma ended up on the floor of Paloma's Pastries in a heap, tears streaming down their faces.

Breakfast with Paloma left Asiri feeling a lot better, but a small knot of anxiety still nestled deep inside her tummy, like a burr stuck in an animal's paw. She was dreading the afternoon when she would see the Amaru—and Dario—again, and at the same time, she absolutely could not wait for it. She alternated between having butterflies at the thought of Dario's face, so close to hers, and vaguely feeling like she might throw up.

Luckily, Doña Iris had decided to send her to an Alpaca farm north of Pisqu to pick up her order of sheared Alpaca fur. Later, Doña Iris promised to show Asiri how to treat it in order to spin it into yarn, which they would then dye. Asiri was very much looking forward to learning a bit more about how Doña Iris made all of her lovely clothes.

The long walk to the farm helped clear her mind and ease her nerves. The day was warm, but the path north skirted the ocean, and there was a cool salty breeze that brushed her hair back from her face and tousled it in the wind. The muffled sounds of the cresting waves against the sandy shore were soothing, and Felipe alternated between flitting between the lush flowers that grew next to the dirt road, and landing on Asiri's shoulders to rest.

Asiri heard the Alpacas before she saw the farm. They were laughing and teasing one another, and she could hear a few doing the Alpaca equivalent of singing a song; reciting their favorite things in order.

Hay, grass, sunshine, water. Running, family, snack time, Gabriel.

They jovially repeated this many times, and Asiri wondered who Gabriel was.

As she approached the main home of the farm, Asiri noticed several other hummingbirds clustered around some bright-looking flowers. With a promise to "be right back," Felipe left his perch on her shoulder and flew away to join them.

Finally, Asiri reached the sprawling, fenced-in fields and the myriad of alpacas in them. Some were tall, with lean elegant necks, others were shorter, with floppy mops of hair over their heads. Some were white, others black, and one had an attractive mixture of the two. There were also alpacas with fur the color of honey and deeper, rich chestnut hues. There were even some llamas roaming the fields with them. Most of the animals seemed to be of an adult age, but a few were clearly very young.

As she approached the main farmhouse, a smiling man exited the building, arms spread wide.

"Bienvenida!" he called out, his voice full of joy. "Welcome to Alpacasa! My name is Gabriel. How can I help you?"

Ah, so this is Gabriel, Asiri thought.

Gabriel was a handsome man a few years older than Asiri. He was slightly shorter than Dario, but much broader. The man was barrel-chested, and his skin was a deeper brown than most of the Pisqu villagers. He boasted a thick beard which framed his angular face, and when he smiled, it was so wide and inviting, Asiri couldn't help but feel happy just being in his vicinity.

"Hola," she greeted him with a grin of her own. "My name is Asiri, Doña Iris sent me to pick up her pedido."

"Claro, claro!" Gabriel said. "I have it in storage. It will take me a few moments to collect it all. Would you like to come in for a drink while you wait?" he asked.

Asiri stole a glance at the alpacas, inching towards the fence nearest to them. "I'd rather stay outside and look at your lovely animals," she admitted.

"Of course!" Gabriel answered. "Here," he said, swinging a satchel over his wide shoulders. "If you give them some carrots, you'll be their best friend for life!" Then walked off towards the back of the farm whistling a happy tune.

Asiri approached the fence, grabbing a few carrots from the bag.

"Hello," she greeted the animals close enough to hear her. "My name is Asiri."

Two alpacas and a llama trotted up to her.

"Hola," the male alpaca said, snatching up a carrot from her hand. "Gracias," he continued, bowing his fuzzy head at her before scampering off.

"Don't mind Santus," the female alpaca said softly. "He isn't very sociable, but he is very kind."

"Yeah, he's just shy," the llama interjected, grabbing a carrot of his own. "But he's a good sort."

"I'm not offended!" Asiri promised them. "You don't have to stay and talk to me, either. It is a beautiful day and I understand that you may have other things to do."

The llama nodded his head. "Yes, some of us are going to have a race!" he told her.

"I hope you win," Asiri told him solemnly. She knew how seriously the alpacas and llamas took their races.

"Gracias, señorita!" he called out, already running back to his friends. The female alpaca stayed. She had long lashes that framed pitch black eyes, a heart-shaped nose, and the most adorable underbite Asiri had ever seen.

"Would you like a carrot too?" Asiri asked, stretching forward with one in her hand. The alpaca ducked her head bashfully.

"Is there an apple? Gabriel sometimes saves me an apple," she told her, voice hopeful.

Asiri dug through the bag, and sure enough, there was an apple wedged in towards the bottom.

"Gracias!" the alpaca said, eyes bright. She gobbled it up quickly. "My name is Suri," she told Asiri.

"Nice to meet you, Suri," Asiri said, leaning over to scratch her behind the ears. "How do you like living here?"

The farm was expansive and well-maintained; the animals seemed plump and happy. But Asiri wanted to make sure that they all felt all right with living in captivity. Some animals were better suited for it than others.

"Gabriel is wonderful to us. He takes good care of us, and plays with us, and makes sure we are all fed and happy," she said.

The knowledge that all the animals were happy and well-cared for made Asiri's heart lift. "I'm glad," she replied honestly.

Suri leaned towards Asiri, her head passing over the fence that separated them.

"Would you like to know a secret?" the alpaca asked.

"Always," Asiri assured her.

"I am going to have a cria!" Suri said, straightening her neck and shuffling from foot to foot in pride.[1]

"A baby!" Asiri gasped. "Oh, how wonderful! Congratulations!"

"Gracias," Suri said happily, her head bobbing up and down as her feet continued to tip tap. "It's my first one."

"That is lovely," Asiri answered, her heart bursting over the alpaca's obvious excitement.

"Would you do me a favor?" Suri asked.

"If I can," Asiri promised.

"Would you please tell Gabriel? He doesn't know that I'm pregnant yet, and I'm already much more hungry. Would you tell him, so he can feed me more? I'm sure that if he knew, he would!" Suri continued.

Asiri hesitated.

Of course, she wanted to help Suri. But how on earth was she going to explain that she somehow knew one of his alpacas was pregnant, even before he did? There was no way she could convince him without betraying her secret. And Asiri really didn't want anyone to know about her gift.

Recently, Asiri considered that it might not be so bad if people knew. Paloma would be understanding, wouldn't she? And she could help Dario, maybe even work in his clinic with him! As much as she loved Doña Iris and her tutelage, in her heart she knew that she would be much happier working with animals.

---

1. Baby alpacas are called "crias."

But then she remembered all the times someone learned of her abilities. How quickly they would expect her to use it to their advantage.

"Convince the stallion to mate with the mare, the foal would be worth a lot of coin."

"Tell the cats to hunt the mice in the barn."

"Train the birds to deliver our messages. Tell them not to stop or rest until they've arrived."

Asiri was sick of it. So many of the demands were impossible, anyway. Just because she could speak to animals didn't mean that they had to listen to her. Some orders she flat out refused for ethical reasons. But no matter what, once people knew what she could do, they wanted to use her. Just like her father used her to make money and further his political ambitions.

But here was Suri, an animal, asking her for help. It was the opposite of everything she had grown up with. How could Asiri let her down?

"Umm," Asiri started, before Gabrial returned with a large bag full of mostly white alpaca fur.

"Here we are," he said, handing her the bundle. Asiri noticed that he had added a thick strap to it, so that she could carry it over her shoulders. "You'll be all right to carry it all the way back?" Gabriel asked her, a note of concern in his voice.

"Yes, I'll be fine, thank you," Asiri answered, then chewed on her lower lip.

"Was there anything else?" Gabriel asked.

Asiri glanced at Suri, who was looking at her expectantly. Asiri cleared her throat. "Well, actually ..." she looked between Suri and Gabriel, back to Suri, then cast her eyes down on the dirt ground.

"No, that's all," she replied quietly, turning to leave. "Gracias."
She felt Suri's disappointed eyes all the way back home.

LLAMA

CHAPTER 18

ASIRI

Hours after she returned from the Alpaca farm, Asiri was still feeling miserable.

Guilt churned in her stomach, making her feel nauseated. She knew that Suri and her cria were in no immediate danger, but she also knew that she let the alpaca down. She kept seeing her sad, soulful eyes radiating betrayal. All Asiri wanted to do was to crawl in bed and hide under the covers all day, but she knew that she had the Amaru counting on her, and she wasn't about to let another creature down today.

"You've been quiet," Felipe said as they walked to the river—well, while she walked. He flew. "Are you nervous to see Dario?"

Felipe hadn't been there when Suri made her request, and she was too ashamed to tell him the real reason she felt so withdrawn.

"Nothing can happen between me and Dario," she reminded him softly.

Felipe flew a quick ring around her head. "If you say so," he replied.

When they reached the Amaru's cave, Dario was already there as usual.

"I'll leave you two alone," Felipe whispered before flitting off. *Traitor.*

Dario jumped up as soon as he saw her approach, and Asiri nervously tucked her hair behind her ear.

"Hola," he said.

"Hola," Asiri repeated.

They stared at each other for a long moment.

"If you're wondering why I look so clean, it's because I left Pepe at the clinic today," Dario joked with a weak chuckle.

"Right," Asiri laughed nervously. *Why was this so awkward?*

"So, shall we?" Dario said, motioning to the Amaru.

"Yes, yes, of course," Asiri sprang forward, and they knelt before the creature.

"I brought more fish," Dario said, motioning to a bag a few meters away. "But this time we will wait to feed him until after we treat his wing."

"Did you hear that, sweetheart?" Asiri cooed. "You have to behave if you want the fish."

Fish, the Amaru repeated.

"Behave," Asiri stressed as they began removing his bandages. The Amaru growled, and both Dario and Asiri froze.

"Help first, then fish," Asiri urged in her strictest, most no-nonsense voice.

The Amaru grumbled.

Behave. Then fish. His voice sounded petulant in her head, but his body relaxed.

Dario looked at Asiri, and with a little shrug, began his work once more. Together, they fell into a rhythm. As Asiri held the Amaru's wing steady, Dario applied salve, his fingers continuously brushing against her own. She shivered at the contact. When re-wrapping the wing, Dario repositioned her fingers to better keep the brace supported. His large hand engulfed Asiri's, his thumb resting gently over her inner wrist to guide her. She imagined what it would be like to have his hand guide her palm over his own body, tugging her closer, moving their interlocked fingers lower, and lower between them ...

"Perfect," Dario said, staring into her eyes.

Asiri startled. "What?" she whispered. *Why was she whispering?*

"We're done," he said equally soft, his hand still over hers. Their shoulders were touching, and Asiri just needed to twist a little more and their faces would be mere inches apart. She could feel his breath on her cheek.

Asiri shifted, leaning into his heat. Dario's head ducked closer to hers ...

Mate? the Amaru asked, looking between them.

"No!" Asiri gasped, recoiling.

"I'm sorry, I'm so sorry!" Dario stuttered, dropping her wrist and pushing to his feet. "Lo siento, dioses, I'm so stupid,"

"No," Asiri groaned, frustrated. She glared at the Amaru, springing to her feet as well. "No, Dario, it's my fault, I—"

Mate, the Amaru repeated, more definitively. Then, Asiri swore the creature grinned at her, before the skies suddenly opened up and assailed them all in a torrential downpour.

It was unlike anything Asiri had ever witnessed. First, it was a bright, beautiful, cloudless day, as it was on most days in Pisqu. Then, in the blink of an eye, the skies turned gray, and she and Dario were being pummeled with some of the most intense rain she had ever experienced.

"Quick!" Dario called, grabbing her by the arm. Together, they did their best to navigate through the deluge until they made it to the base of an enormous tree. Its canopy was lush and thick, sheltering them from the majority of the downpour. But the violence in which the rain beat against the sprawling leaves made it feel like the world was shaking apart around them.

Mirroring the leaves, Asiri began to tremble. She was completely soaked, as was Dario. Under the cool shade of the tree, the wet clothing drew little shivers from her body. She crossed her arms over her chest to stave off the cold, but to no avail.

"I'm sorry," Dario said suddenly, having to raise his voice over the torrent.

Asiri glanced up at him in surprise.

"Before, I'm sorry. I didn't mean to make you uncomfortable." He was the one who looked uncomfortable, and sad. Asiri was heartbroken that she had put that expression on his face.

"There is nothing to be sorry about," she told him, but he shook his head.

"You clearly didn't want to. You said no." He hesitated. "I misunderstood your interest. It won't happen again."

"I *did* want to," Asiri blurted out, shocking herself. She knew that she shouldn't have wanted to kiss him, that wanting him in any way was dangerous. But dioses knew she did.

"Then why ..." he started, eyes a mixture of hopeful and confused.

Asiri shrugged. She couldn't explain why she had said no, not without lying or revealing her secret. So, she simply repeated, "I did want to—I *have* wanted to." Then, with a shuddering breath, she said, "I still want to."

Dario stared at her for a long time without saying anything. He stared at her for so long that Asiri's body became flooded with mortification. Had she misunderstood? Was it too late? Did he change his mind? The skies continued to pour, and Asiri's body became wracked with another shiver. It seemed to break Dario out of his stupor.

"You're shaking," he murmured, his voice almost swallowed up by the rain. He moved towards her, then stopped. "Is it all right if I—can I—touch you?" he asked tentatively.

Asiri walked straight up to him and folded herself into his chest.

Dario's arms wrapped around her, his thick biceps covering her shoulders all the way down to just above her butt. He tucked her head underneath his chin and she curled her own arms around him, his back so broad that she could barely reach his shoulder blades. One of his palms dragged up and down the wet fabric of her shirt, warming her up in more ways than one. His thighs burned against hers, flush against her legs and hips. His stomach and chest were crushing her breasts, and the sensation was indescribable, the pressure easing the ache that had been driving her crazy since the moment she saw him.

Almost instantly, Asiri's body became filled with a desperate need. After denying her attraction to him for so long, the incredible awareness of finally having him so close made her body react with a pleasure so powerful her knees buckled. Dario felt her body tremble, and mistaking it for cold, he cradled her head and backed her against the trunk of the tree, sheltering her body with as much of his own as possible.

The tickling sensation of his breath on her neck drew a tiny whimper from her throat. "Shhh," he whispered almost inaudibly into her ear. He pressed impossibly closer to her, causing another tremor to quake through her body. "It's all right," he continued. "The rain will let up in a few minutes."

In a few minutes? In a few minutes, Asiri would strip the clothes from her body and beg him to take her. The thought of being naked with him stole another moan from her mouth. Unable to contain herself, she dug her fingers into his waist and buried her face in his chest. And that's when she felt it. Dario tried to shift back a fraction, but she felt the stirring of his desire against her stomach. She pulled him closer again and felt him growing hard against her.

Dario hissed out a breath. "Shit, I'm sorry ..." he murmured, but a strangled moan cut his words off as Asiri arched against him.

Oh dioses, she thought, and did it again.

This time he reacted by pushing back against her and dropping his head to her shoulder with a gasp, his breath hot against the sensitive crook of her neck. She couldn't help it. Unable to stop, she snuck her fingers underneath his shirt and dragged her nails up over the hard, rough ridges and planes of his back. The contact stirred Dario into action. Using his foot to open her legs wider, he responded by bending his knees and aligning himself against her core. Feeling his arousal against her center, Asiri gasped and threw her head back against the trunk, the cool wood a brilliant contrast to the heat radiating off Dario's body. Greedily, she rubbed herself against him, panting and gasping with pleasure. Dario's hand reached down to grab her ass firmly, moving her even harder and tighter against him. With his other hand, he pushed her hair off her face to stare at her in amazement. She bit her lip and whimpered.

"Dioses," he mumbled right before crushing his lips to hers. It was no sweet, hesitant first kiss. They were too far gone to begin slowly. His tongue swept into her mouth, demanding, and she responded with fervor of her own until all they were was a wild frenzy of lips and teeth and tongue. Asiri's fingers tangled in his hair, her other hand still underneath his shirt, trying to touch as much skin as possible. She could feel his cock twitch against her, and she moved against him harder, her body shamelessly trying to find some relief. Dario brought his hand up to cup her cheek, nipping at her lower lip.

Then, just as suddenly as the rain began, it stopped completely. Dario and Asiri broke away from one another with a jolt, the sudden quiet feeling louder than the thundering rain had been. Asiri could feel her nipples tight and hard underneath her shirt, and she was panting. Dario looked flushed, his lips plump and wet. Asiri did her best not to look down below his waist.

The reality of the situation crashed into her, dousing her lust more effectively than the rain had. What had she been thinking? Hadn't she decided that this was exactly the last thing that she should be doing? Avoiding Dario's eyes, she began making her way back to the path to Pisqu. Her legs felt weak, and she nearly stumbled over a root before righting herself quickly. Dario reached out for her, but she waved him off.

"I'm fine," she said. "I have to go. I'm sorry." She still couldn't meet his eyes. "I have to go."

She made it ten steps before she stopped. Not trusting herself to look at Dario, she kept her back to him.

"You know Gabriel? Who owns the Alpaca farm?" she asked him.

"Yes …" he replied, drawing out the word.

"Do you treat his animals?" she asked.

"I do," he said. "But what does—"

"One of his females, Suri, is pregnant," Asiri interrupted him. "Next time you're there, maybe you could check on her."

Then she left, not looking back.

The entire way, she could hear the Amaru's laughter inside her head.

MONKEY FROG/
RANA KAMBÓ

CHAPTER 19

DARIO

D ario was confused.

He felt elated, turned on, a little breathless, but mostly confused.

He and Asiri had kissed! Her mouth, all soft and sweet and giving underneath his own, haunted him. He had held her in his arms. She had kissed him back. Dioses, it felt like she wanted to do more than kiss him back, and Dario clutched the flesh over his galloping heart at the very thought of it.

But then, when the strange, other-worldly rain had stopped, she had sprung away from him like he was diseased. Like she couldn't wait to be far from his presence. Her demeanor shifted from blazing hot to arctic cold in the blink of an eye.

Again.

Then Asiri had mentioned Gabriel, the owner of the Alpaca farm, and Dario felt like someone had punched him in the gut. Was she in a relationship with him? It seemed unlikely, Asiri had only been in Pisqu for a few weeks, and she had spent most of her time between working for Doña Iris and caring for the Amaru. But perhaps they had known each other from before she moved to town?

Dario didn't know what to do. Asiri was incredible. She was sweet, kind, and caring. He could tell she felt a dedication to helping animals, even if she did seem a bit wary around some of them. She was beautiful and soft. And when her body was flush against his, when she moved like she did, and whimpered into his mouth ...

No, Dario thought, blood rushing south. *I can't get distracted. She ran off, and I need to figure out why.*

Determined, Dario changed directions and started heading towards the Alpaca farm. His sister could look after the animals a little while longer; he needed to get some answers.

A few hours later, Dario arrived at Alpacasa, and his mood was instantly lighter. He loved alpacas and llamas. Sure, they could kick and spit sometimes, but deep down, he knew they were mostly sweethearts. Some made their way to the fence as he approached, likely remembering his previous visits to the farm.

"No snacks today, my friends," he told them, patting a few on the head while they sniffed at his clothes and pockets, making sure he wasn't lying. Dario laughed.

He noticed Suri, the alpaca that Asiri had mentioned, walking up to him shyly. With a quick hop of the fence, he crossed to her, patting and stroking her soothingly. She didn't appear outwardly pregnant, but Dario did a more thorough exam.

Sure enough, Suri was expecting a cria. It was early days, but he could tell.

How could Asiri have known? If he could barely tell, how could a woman with no animal healing experience have figured it out? Before even Gabriel, who lived and worked with his animals every day?

Speaking of Gabriel, Dario noticed that he was across the field and making his way to him. Dario usually liked the man. He was friendly and intelligent and good to his animals. He always took Dario's suggestions to heart, and the few times he was free enough to take a break and come to the village, they had shared a few cervezas. But now, with the thought that he might be involved with Asiri, he couldn't help but feel resentful of his annoying farmer's muscles, and his dumb broad shoulders, and that damned thick beard that framed his stupidly handsome face.

Gabriel raised his hand up in greeting, and Dario forced himself to smile and wave back.

"Dario!" Gabriel said, reaching him and pulling him in for a quick, back-thumping hug. "I didn't expect you today! Everything well, amigo?" he asked.

Dario did his best to swallow his irritation.

"Yes, yes, todo bien," he answered, his voice tight. "Just thought I would stop by and check on your friends," he continued, motioning to the pack of animals that were surrounding the two of them.

"That is very kind of you," Gabriel replied with a grin. "Anything I should know about?"

Dario suddenly wondered if the answer to his puzzle was simple, and Gabriel had simply told Asiri about the pregnancy. Jealousy burned in his gut, and he had a sudden vision of tripping Gabriel right into a pile of Alpaca poop. Instead, he forced himself to ask; "Did you know that Suri is pregnant?"

Gabriel's mouth dropped open, and he spun towards Suri. "No! Really?" A grin pulled his cheeks so high his eyes were suddenly slivers in his face.

"You didn't know?" Dario asked suspiciously.

"No idea!" he replied, running his hands over Suri's flank and belly. "How far along is she?"

"Not far, it's early still," Dario responded, feeling relieved. So, Gabriel hadn't told Asiri.

But then, how did Asiri know?

He pushed the question from his mind and forced himself to focus on the task at hand. "It wouldn't hurt to start feeding her a little more hay, oats, peas, and such that she can't just graze for. And I know you know the signs to look out for, but let's go over them again together now."

Dario spent the next quarter of an hour reminding Gabriel on how to care for a pregnant alpaca. Then, because he was there, he spent some time looking over the other animals, including Gabriel's hairless dog Lalo, who showed his appreciation by smothering him with slobbery kisses just like the puppy in his office did. It made him laugh.

By the time Dario was done, his mood was much improved, but he still didn't know if Gabriel and Asiri were together, and couldn't think of any good way to broach the subject. Finally, he stifled his pride and regarded Gabriel once more.

"Been to town recently?" he asked, and Gabriel shook his head.

"Not in a long time, amigo," he answered with a sigh. "The farm has been taking up so much of my time. I barely get any breaks at all, so going into Pisqu hasn't been an option recently."

"Oh, so you haven't met the new addition?" Dario asked, his voice deliberately casual.

Gabriel frowned a little, then his face lit up. "Oh, you mean Doña Iris's new hire? Asiri? Qué bonita la chica, no?"

Jealousy flared hot and angry through Dario's chest, incinerating his prior good mood to ash. *Of course, Asiri was pretty,* he thought. But he resented Gabriel for acknowledging it so casually.

"So, you have met," he bit out tersely.

Gabriel seemed oblivious to Dario's fiery mood. "Only once," the farmer admitted. "Just this morning, she came by to pick up Doña Iris's order. Seemed to like the animals. It's always nice to know more people with an appreciation for animals."

Dario's shoulders relaxed by a fraction. So they weren't together, couldn't be, if they had just met. Dario's first instinct was to feel relieved, but then confusion returned, knocking his relief to the side. If she wasn't with Gabriel, then why had she left so quickly after they had kissed? And why did it seem like she liked him one moment, and couldn't wait to be rid of him the next?

Gabriel thanked him once again for stopping by, and Dario made his way back into town, his head swimming with questions. He thought long and hard about his time with Asiri and their interactions. By the time he was home, he had decided something.

He liked Asiri.

He *really* liked Asiri.

He hadn't realized just how lonely he was until she appeared like a vision from his dreams. He thought he was content with his family and his animals and his practice. But he realized he was living in the coldness of complacency and she had come in like the dawn, melting away all of his excuses about how he was perfectly fine on his own. And now that he was aware of the gaping hole in his life, he was going to do everything he could to fill it; with her. He would court her, officially, and do his absolute best to prove just how good they could be together. If she was uncertain about her feelings towards him, then he would respect her and give her space, but until he was absolutely sure that she didn't want him, he was going to do everything in his power to win her heart. She was worth every second of uncertainty.

BLACK CAIMAN / CAIMÁN NEGRO

CHAPTER 20

ASIRI

Asiri sat at the edge of the ocean, a basket full of indigo plants on the sand next to her. Her feet were bare, and every so often the foamy crest would tickle her toes, only to disappear backward into the endless blue once more. She knew that the sea deserved her respect, but on days like today, it felt like a friend, tugging gently at her ankles and daring her to wade in deeper.

But Asiri felt too distracted to entertain a swim.

You've made such a mess of things, she thought to herself.

Asiri didn't know what to do. When she had left Casa de Murmuros, things had been so clear. She wanted a new life, a fresh start, somewhere where no one knew her secret, and couldn't use it for their own gain. She wanted to live somewhere where she could just be Asiri, rather than the girl with the gift, the creature communer, the weird outsider.

But then she had met Paloma, and Doña Iris, and Dario. Keeping that part of herself hidden from them, no matter what her reasons, felt like lying to them. And she didn't like the feeling.

Would it really be so bad? she thought. *If I told them?*

She imagined Paloma's wide eyes, asking her questions about her upbringing, and her time in the pachas. She could tell her about the gigantic spread of food that Pachamama set out in Kay Pacha, with all her harvests and grains. They could sit in Paloma's Pastries, and Asiri could relay all the jacamar bird's best gossip as they laughed and sipped on café.

Then she thought of confessing to Doña Iris how much the animals helped her in gathering materials, how they knew the best spots to find flowers and insects and snails for her dyes. She thought of the serious, pragmatic woman accepting help from the animals, and showing Asiri how to make happy, colorful clothing in their free time.

And she envisioned telling Dario, admitting that she could help him to better heal his patients by explaining just what ailed them, where they hurt, and what symptoms they were experiencing. They could work together, the two of them in his clinic, helping more animals than ever. He would be astonished and grateful! So grateful that he would pull her into his strong arms, tell her how wonderful she was, and kiss her again and again and again ...

Asiri shook her head to clear it. They were pretty fantasies, but that was all that they were. Things hardly worked that well in real life. The people of Pisqu were superstitious. Paloma might suddenly start to fear her if she confessed. She could accuse Asiri of having animals spy on her, like Usuela—a member of Casa de Murmuros—had several years ago. Instead of being impressed with the help her animal friends gave her, Doña Iris could accuse Asiri of lying to her, using the animals to do her chores for her instead of working hard herself.

And Dario ... she didn't want to begin to think of how Dario could react. What if her secret stole the friendly smile from his face? What if he never again looked at her how he had the day before? Right before he had held her, right before he had backed her into the tree and covered her body with his own?

Asiri could stand it if she couldn't have him. She would survive never kissing him again, if it at least meant keeping him as a friend. What she wouldn't be able to survive was his indifference, his fear, or his hatred.

It's too risky, Asiri decided. She couldn't tell them, any of them. Which meant she had to put some distance between herself and Dario.

With a sigh, Asiri rose from the warm beach. More than she would ever admit, her heart hurt at the prospect of never being in Dario's arms again. But at least he would still be in her life. Her heart would recover, and they would become friends. It was for the best.

Once she made her decision, the last thing that Asiri wanted to do was face Dario. What would she say? How would he react after yesterday? Asiri wanted to wade into the ocean and float weightlessly until the sea carried all of her worries and anxieties out of her body, then take a nice long nap on the sand.

But it was not just Dario who was expecting her. The Amaru needed her help, and she wasn't about to let the creature down. She would not allow her cowardice to get in the way of tending a wounded animal. She wouldn't fail him the way she had Suri.

With a heavy sigh, she turned and walked toward the forest.

To Asiri's astonishment, by the time she reached the Amaru's cave, Dario was already finished rewrapping its injured wing.

"Hola!" he greeted her, his voice as cheery as his smile. "I arrived early today, and he was very good. I managed to treat and bandage him by myself."

"Oh," Asiri responded, a feeling very much like disappointment settling inside her bones. "I'll just ... I'll go then."

"Espera!" Dario called out, standing up.

Dioses, he's tall, Asiri thought dumbly.

"I want to show you something," he said

Asiri hesitated. This was precisely the sort of situation that she should avoid. Hadn't she just decided that nothing more could happen between her and Dario? The last thing that she needed was an afternoon alone with him.

"I don't think—" she started.

"We have the afternoon, right?" Dario interrupted, stepping closer to her, his eyes wide and dark and intent on her face. "I promise you'll like it."

Oh, I'm sure I'd like it, a rebellious voice in Asiri's head said. Ignoring it, she shook her head. "I really should get back-"

"Por favor."

It was said quietly. He wasn't pushing her, wasn't insisting. He just said please.

Against her better judgment, Asiri felt herself nod.

"Ok."

They didn't speak as Dario led her deeper into the forest. Asiri's heart was pounding hard in her chest, and several times she nearly turned around to head back to Pisqu. But the problem was that she didn't *want* to go back. She wanted to be there with Dario. No matter what her mind had decided, her body, and her heart, kept pulling her towards him.

Suddenly, Dario turned to her and grinned. "We're here," he said, and grabbed her hand, pulling her through a large thicket.

Asiri gasped. In front of them was the base of a small mountain, barely more than a hill really, but one that contained another wide and happy river. When the water reached the edge of the mount, it cascaded over its side, creating a beautiful, crashing waterfall. It wasn't the largest waterfall that Asiri had ever seen—which explained why she hadn't heard it before they reached its base— but it was a stunning one, nonetheless.

The water was so clear it looked teal in color and emptied into a small lake. Bright green plants and shrubs, and wildflowers in colors of oranges, pinks, purples and yellows surrounded it. There were birds, frogs, foxes, and other wild animals, but most were quietly relaxing near the lake's edge, or spoke softly enough that the falls muffled their voices. It was tranquil and serene, and absolutely perfect.

"It's beautiful," Asiri told Dario in awe.

"Beautiful," Dario agreed. When Asiri turned to look at him, she realized that he was staring right at her. She was suddenly very aware that they were still holding hands, and with a blush she dropped his and stepped quickly to the side.

Dario seemed undeterred. With a mischievous grin, he pulled his shirt over his head.

"What are you doing?" Asiri squeaked as toned, tanned flesh came into view. *A lot* of toned, tan flesh.

"We can't come all this way and not go for a swim!" he declared.

Asiri did her best to keep her eyes on his face, but her traitorous eyes fell to the large expanse of his chest. Swallowing hard, she shook her head.

"I didn't bring—"

But before she could finish, Dario fished out a dark blue tunic from his pack.

"Something to swim in? Don't worry, you can borrow this," he said.

It looked to be one of his own, long enough that it would hit Asiri right below the knee. It was perfectly acceptable, and yet Asiri hesitated.

"Do you not want to swim?" Dario asked her, disappointment in his voice.

Asiri looked back at the crystalline lake. She *did* want to swim. She very much wanted to swim. She could do this, couldn't she? Spend time with Dario as a friend?

"Ok," she finally answered, and Dario's smile evaporated any doubt or worry in her mind.

"You can change over there," he said, pointing to a thick cluster of trees. Asiri accepted the tunic from his outstretched hand and scurried over to them. As soon as the rocks concealed her, she could hear a loud splash behind her. She closed her eyes, doing her best not to imagine him wet and flushed from the sun. Quickly, she discarded her clothing and pulled on the tunic. As predicted, it covered more than enough skin.

Stepping out towards the lake once again, she looked for Dario in the water, but couldn't find him. Frowning, she left her clothing in a pile on top of his pack, and stepped to the edge.

"Dario?" she called out, but still couldn't see him. Was he under the water? She waded in, trying to find a shadow underneath the rippling pool, but could still not see anything. Nerves rustled in her chest.

"Dario?" she repeated, shivering as the water reached her belly. "Hola?"

No answer. With a deep breath, she submerged herself entirely, squinting underwater, trying to find his familiar form. She broke to the surface once more, panting.

"Dario!" she yelled, worried now.

Asiri nearly sank back down underwater when Dario's face suddenly appeared from behind the falls, completely unharmed. He grinned mischievously at her.

"Coming?" he called over the rush of the water, then disappeared again.

Grumbling about inconsiderate men, she paddled towards the falls. With a gulping breath, she broke through, and suddenly found herself on the opposite side of the waterfall in a small blue cave.

"Oh," Asiri gasped appreciatively, pushing her hair away from her face. Dario was sitting on a large rock, slow droplets of water tracing patterns into his bare torso. Despite the water, Asiri's mouth felt dry. She made her way deeper into the cave, the water becoming more and more shallow until she was stepping out of the small pool and next to Dario's rock. She looked at him and paused.

Dario's chest was rising and falling rapidly, his fingers digging into the edge of the stone. His eyes roved slowly over her swept back hair, down her face, stopping for a second on her lips. She licked them nervously. Then he continued his perusal down her body, and Asiri could see the muscles in his stomach clench.

The tunic that he had leant her still hit below her knees, but had become completely plastered to her curves. The wet cloth and the coolness of the cave made her nipples pucker, straining against the fabric. Dario's slow, burning gaze over her silhouette caused a deep pang of lust to shoot between her legs, and she pressed her thighs together to try to alleviate the aching throb of it. It was so potent it was nearly painful, and in that moment Asiri wanted nothing more than for Dario to follow the path his eyes had cut with his hands instead.

Asiri watched as Dario dragged his eyes away from her body with a gulp. "This is called a 'rock shelter,'" he explained, his voice tight. He wouldn't meet her eye. "They form because the water from the falls erodes the rocks behind it, causing the area to re-recede," he stammered. "It happens because the force of the falling water causes churning at its base, where the water hits the pool, and it slowly wears away the stone over time. Over a very, very long time, of course."

He finally looked at her again, embarrassment flickering over his features. "Sorry," he mumbled. "I sometimes talk too much. I know you've noticed."

"I like to hear you talk," Asiri told him honestly, and watched as doubt shadowed his eyes. "Really," she insisted.

Dario hesitated. "It seemed like you might have found it irritating, at times."

Asiri's heart clenched with guilt. All this time, she thought that her actions had made her seem like a madwoman. She hadn't considered that Dario would believe her behavior was somehow his fault. She remembered Belinda's words in the Tienda del Tejido, and wondered just how often Dario withstood the cruel opinions of people like her.

"I think you're brilliant," she blurted out. "I am always interested in what you have to say. If I ever made you feel otherwise, I am so sorry."

Relief so fragile, it was almost painful to look at crossed Dario's face.

Pulled by an invisible and inexplicable force, Asiri stepped towards him, unsure of why, only that his expression did nothing to ease the tightness in her heart. She was nearly to him when she suddenly slipped on one of the slick rocks. For a breathless moment she was tumbling forward, afraid she was going to smash her head on one of the larger cave stones, when suddenly she felt herself engulfed by warm, wet heat.

Dario's arms were around her waist, gripping her tightly against his chest. Her bare legs pressed up against his, the fine hair on his calves tickling her oversensitive flesh. She had managed to throw her arms around his neck and was now clutching at him, staring at him with wide-eyed surprise and fear, which morphed very suddenly into need.

"Are you—" he started, before Asiri gripped the back of his head and crushed his lips to hers.

Dario's grip tightened for a quick, instinctual second, hard and bruising against her hips. Then he lifted one hand to grasp Asiri's neck, holding her in place while he adjusted their angle and slipped his tongue inside of her mouth.

Asiri moved her own against his greedily, her body a live flame of molten desire. She curled her right leg around his and he followed it with his hand, palming her over her clothes from hip to calf. She felt him growing hard against her lower stomach and she rocked into him, drawing out a growling, "*fuck*" from his lips against her mouth. The hand around her neck slipped down to cup her breast, and she whimpered as he traced the hard peak of her nipple through the wet fabric. His mouth moved to her chin, her cheek, her ear, then down to her neck, while Asiri continued to rock herself against the hard length of him.

With another curse, Dario released her breast and leg to grab the fleshy rounds of her ass, lifting her against him. She opened her legs, causing the tunic to ride up to her hips, and he sat back down on the rock, placing her aching, wet heat right where she needed it. A sharp moan escaped her as he used his grip to move her against the straining fabric of his shorts, the fat head of his cock dragging deliciously over her clit again, and again, and again.

Asiri whimpered, clawing at his shoulders, biting his lower lip, completely mad with need. Dario grabbed a fistful of her hair and arched her back so that he could close his hungry mouth over her breast. She could feel his lips, his tongue, *dioses his teeth* through the fabric, but it wasn't enough. Her hand snaked between the two of them, their bodies pressed together so tight that her small palm could barely fit through. Then she found him, hot and hard and pulsing against her fingers.

"I can't—*fuck*—I need," Dario gasped before grasping the edges of her tunic and drawing it off her, flinging the offending material to the side. She sat astride him, naked, wet, and aching, brown nipples straining for his attention, and her legs splayed wide open and on display over him.

"I need," he repeated, turning them both so that her bare ass hit the stone. She yelped at the contact, but before she could comment, Dario was kneeling between her legs, his tongue tracing a pattern from her knee to the inside of her thigh.

With a strangled whimper, Asiri rested on her elbows, her head tilted back, back arched and hips rolling.

"Please," she whispered, not even caring that she was begging for it. She gripped his hair, and he looked up at her, his lips swollen and glistening. "*Please*," she repeated.

Asiri watched as the restraint behind Dario's eyes snapped, darkening with promise. With an iron grip, he swung one of her legs over his shoulder then buried his face in her sex.

Asiri's gasping cry of pleasure reverberated against the cave's walls, and she felt an answering groan from between her legs. Dario's thumbs parted her folds and his tongue swept over her from bottom to top, where he stopped and *sucked*. Asiri's thighs clutched at the sides of his head and she trembled, but Dario didn't let up. He swirled his tongue in small circles around her clit, then moved down to lap at her juices, only to come back and suckle on her some more. Asiri was arching, undulating, alternating between clutching at her aching breasts to gripping Dario's hair. When he slipped two of his fingers inside of her and curled them, Asiri bowed up so hard she was surprised that she didn't hit the roof of the cave. He moved his fingers faster, locking his mouth around her clit.

"Yes, yes, yes," she repeated. His fingers fucked her faster, and when she felt the barest scrape of his teeth against her clit, her world shattered into a million pieces. She was back in the center of the universe, but this time there was blinding pleasure as well as light, and she screamed from the force of it. Then, little by little, she was pulled back together, her mind returning to her body, which was still quaking from the aftershocks, thighs sore from clenching them so hard, her ass cold and clammy against the damp stone. As she struggled to catch her breath, she felt soft, sweet kisses pepper her hips, then her stomach, to below her breasts. Gentle hands slipped under her back and head, and then Dario was there, braced over her, kissing her lips. She shivered against him, managing to bring up her hand to cup his cheek. Then he pulled back and smiled at her.

Asiri smiled back, dazed. Then it occurred to her. "You," she said, motioning below his waist. "I can—" but he interrupted her with a searing kiss. Despite the mind-numbing orgasm she just had, she felt herself growing wet again.

"There was nothing in this world that could have kept me from finishing once I got my mouth on you," he admitted to her after pulling away. "I was done for the second I tasted you." He punctuated his words by reaching down to cup her. Asiri keened, arching into his touch.

"Still so wet," Dario whispered against her neck, tracing her lower lips with his fingers. Asiri gasped. "Still so hot," he mumbled against her breasts, his fingers gliding against her clit with feather light touches.

"Dario," she sighed, and she felt his mouth pause against her nipple. He looked up at her, his gaze partially obscured by his hair. She gently pushed it away from his eyes. "Say that again," he demanded.

"Hmm?" she murmured, trying to pull him closer to her. He stopped moving, and she frowned.

"Say my name again, just like that," he asked, sucking her nipple into his mouth and pulling. Asiri gasped.

"Dario," she repeated. "Dario, por favor."

With an approving growl, he moved his mouth to her other nipple, and rewarded her by slipping his fingers back inside of her, angling his palm against her already aching clit. She clutched at his shoulders and he tongued her neck, her breasts, kissed her mouth and sucked on her lips, all the while his fingers bringing her closer and closer to shattering again. When she did, he swallowed up her desperate cries and held her until she stopped shaking.

Then Dario stared at her with a look more naked than Asiri was, and her treacherous heart tumbled in her chest.

BUSH DOG /
SACHA PERRO

CHAPTER 21

ASIRI

Shit, shit, shit, Asiri thought.

She had just had sex with Dario. Sure, only his fingers had been inside of her, and his tongue—*dioses his tongue*—but it was sex, nonetheless. Which was exactly what she had convinced herself she wasn't supposed to do.

They were quiet as they walked back towards the Amaru. Dario wanted to check on him one more time before heading back into town. If he noticed her spiraling trepidation, he didn't mention it. In fact, he seemed content to give her time and space to sort out her feelings.

But what *was* she feeling?

Good, she thought. *I am feeling good.*

She felt light, and boneless, and more relaxed than she had felt ... well, ever, really. It was astounding, and she knew it was because of him. No other sexual encounter had ever left her feeling so perfect. Except, it wasn't just the sex. Even though Dario was very, very good at it, it was him. It was Dario. He had a way of making her feel beautiful, desirable, and cherished. She liked it.

She wanted it.

So why can't I have it? she asked herself.

The answer was clear. It was the same obstacle that she kept coming up against, over and over again. She needed to keep her gift a secret. She was unwilling to share it with anyone, not even Dario. In many ways, especially not Dario. She couldn't be sure that he wouldn't use her for it. What if he kept her around just because she was useful to him and the practice? It didn't seem like something that he would do. He seemed like a good person, but she couldn't be sure. How well did she know him?

He just had his head buried between your legs, chica, she thought. *I think it's safe to say that you know him fairly well.*

She chanced a glance at him, his skin just a touch darker after their afternoon in the sun. He had put his shirt back on, but after touching his wet skin and then drying wrinkles had formed in several places. He walked unhurriedly next to her, whistling softly.

He looked happy.

Asiri realized that she was happy, too.

Maybe I can have him anyway, she thought. *Maybe we can be together, and he doesn't have to know about my gift. I can continue to keep it a secret...*

and continue to touch him.

A pang of lust hit Asiri, so potent she nearly stumbled. Not just lust, she realized, but *want.* She wanted Dario, not just his body and his mouth and his touch, but Dario. She wanted to be with him, and spend time with him, and get to know him better. She didn't want to deny herself what she wanted anymore.

With a deep breath, she reached out and took his hand. Dario's face erupted into a smile larger than she had ever seen before, and he tugged her closer. He didn't say a word, just held her hand with that stupid grin on his face all the way back to the Amaru.

When Asiri returned to Pisqu—still flushed from the goodbye kiss Dario had given her at her door—Doña Iris called her down to the Tienda.

"It is time to learn more of the art of el tejido," the older woman said.

Asiri brightened. She had wanted a chance to learn to make her own clothing since she had first come to Pisqu! The thought of being able to fashion something for herself that she actually liked, something with color and pattern, made her already full heart feel close to bursting.

"Before you can learn to make fabric," Doña Iris informed her, "you need to learn how to get the yarn ready. Bring me the bag of alpaca fur."

Asiri scrambled to do what she was told.

"Now, this is already washed and cleaned," Doña Iris continued, "so we need to prepare it."

With a fat, bristly brush, Doña Iris showed Asiri how to card and comb the fur so that all the fibers faced the same direction, combing again and again until only the finest fibers remained. Then, with a quick twist of her fingers, Doña Iris attached the end of the fiber to a spindle, spinning as she fed more and more fibers as she went along, eventually creating long pieces of yarn.

"It does not need to be washed again," Doña Iris explained, "as alpaca fur does not have many oils. But these are now ready to be dyed in the vats. That part of the process, you know," she continued.

Asiri nodded. The yellow, pink and lilac yarn she repeatedly dyed over the week had finally achieved the right pigment. To her surprise, Doña Iris took out that very yarn, already wrapped in tight little bundles.

"Ven," Doña Iris instructed her, making her way back to the main part of the tienda, then folding herself down onto the ground. "You would have to wait for the yarn you just prepared, but I will show you the next step with yarn that is ready."

Doña Iris's loom was attached to one of the two pillars in the center of the store. The long threads stretched from where they attached to a high pillar, down towards the wooden contraption. Doña Iris adjusted the strap to rest behind her back, pulling the wool taught.

For the next hour, Doña Iris explained the different parts of the loom to Asiri, and what each individual wooden rod and stick did. She showed her the process in which dozens of individual pieces of yarn were combined, picked up, dropped, or woven to make patterns.

By the time she declared that they "had done enough for the day," Asiri's head was reeling. She felt simultaneously impressed and exhausted. She already knew how much work went into preparing and coloring the yarn, but she didn't realize how much more she needed to learn before being able to fashion it all into fabric! While her admiration of Doña Iris soared, Asiri couldn't help but feel slightly disappointed. If it took this long just to prepare the materials, how long would it take her to learn how to make clothing for herself?

"Muy bien, chica," Doña Iris said as they were packing up. "You did well. In fact, you have been doing well this entire week. I have accomplished so much more than usual because of your help."

Asiri felt tears prickle the backs of her eyes, but she blinked them away. In her short experience with the woman, Asiri knew that Doña Iris was reserved in expressing her approval, which made her praise even more special.

"Thank you for taking the time to teach me!" she beamed at the older woman, who just brushed her off with the wave of her hand.

"One more thing," Doña Iris said, grabbing a bundle from one of the shop's shelves. "You can't be working for me and look like a supay," she said.[1]

Asiri looked down at her bland, dark clothing and grimaced.

"I know," she sighed. "When I have enough, I will buy something new, I promise -" she began, but Doña Iris cut her off.

"Don't be ridiculous, you work for me. Here," the woman said, tossing a package at Asiri, who caught it just in time.

Opening up the wrapped bundle, Asiri gasped, and the tears that she had so valiantly tried not to shed began streaming down her face. Doña Iris had given her new clothes! There was a soft blue blouse and shawl in rainbow colors. The skirt was still black, Asiri realized, but hemmed in pink with yellow stripes and a spattering of flowers embroidered in sunny colors ran across the bottom. She even supplied Asiri with some long, colorful scraps of fabric that she could braid into her hair.

"Now *that* is how you wear black," Doña Iris said, her voice haughty, surprising a watery chuckle from Asiri.

---

1. A supay is a demonio, or demon, of Ukhu Pacha.

"It's too much," Asiri sniffed, but Doña Iris waved her off again.

"You're a good girl," she answered simply. "You deserve pretty things." And with that, she walked out of the store, leaving Asiri with wet cheeks and a very full heart.

VISCACHA

CHAPTER 22

DARIO

D ario was so happy he felt like he was going to lift off the
very ground and float up into the sky.

What happened in the cave was by far the best moment of
Dario's life. Nothing would ever surpass the experience of touching Asiri, of seeing her naked, and wet, and open in front of him,
of hearing her let out those sexy, little panting whimpers as he
touched her with his hands, and his mouth, and his tongue. She
felt so good and tasted even better. All he had to do was press his
palm over himself as she came undone against him, and he had
toppled right over that same ledge to join her. It felt incredible. He
couldn't even find it in himself to be embarrassed about it—Asiri
certainly hadn't seemed to mind.

Afterward, she had withdrawn a bit, and it took everything in
Dario's power not to panic. Did she regret it? Would she pull away
from him? He wanted to ask her. He wanted to ask how she felt
about what happened, and how she felt about him. He wanted to
tell her how he was feeling, that he felt nothing but gratitude for
every little moment in his life that had led him to the river on the
day he first saw her. That he had been slowly drowning in apathy
and that her presence breathed new life into his lungs. He wanted

to tell her that if she let him, he would spend the rest of his life proving himself worthy of her.

But he had said none of it. Instead, though it ached with every fiber of his being, Dario had given her space. He didn't want to pressure her in any way, so he forced himself to stay quiet, to not overwhelm her with his feelings while she figured out her own. She remained quiet as they dressed and made their way back to the Amaru.

His heart had nearly burst in relief when it turned out to be the right thing to do, because she had eventually taken his hand in hers.

Dario's palm burned at the memory, and he rubbed his hand over his heart. Sure, she had dropped it once they reached Pisqu, but had let him kiss her softly at the backdoor of Doña Iris's shop. Tonight, he would go back to Tienda del Tejido and ask her out properly. They would share a meal, maybe at Jose's taverna, and they could get to know each other better away from the pressures of tending to a semidios. He could make her smile, make her laugh ... and then hopefully make her come again.

Dario grinned as he walked back into his practice. Today was going to be a good day.

Today has not been a good day, Dario thought as he admitted yet another patient into a cage. A fluffy rabbit named Pirolin who no longer wished to eat. She was only the last in a long line of patients that greeted him once he had returned, a frazzled Tamya glaring at him.

"Where have you been?" she demanded, before nearly wrenching his arm out of his socket by dragging him into the building to a lobby full of both humans and animals. "People have been waiting forever!"

First, there was the parakeet with the most foul-smelling stool he had ever had the misfortune of experiencing. Then the elderly dog, who had a large splinter in his paw. There was a goat who had gotten into a fight with another goat and had a bleeding gash above his eye. Then the nervous pet owners of a pregnant cat who wanted her checked out, even though she was doing perfectly fine. Dario even had to make a house call to a nearby farm to check on one of their donkeys, who would not stop braying.

By the time he placed Pirolin in her cage, it was very late, and Dario was very tired.

Tamya had stayed to help him, dioses bless her, and they had taken turns washing and changing in the practice's private baths. Dario would never regret that investment! He had just settled into his desk chair when Tamya walked into his office, hair wet and holding two cervezas. The chimú dog—who Dario was starting to get very tempted to name—wagged her tail happily at seeing Tamya, but didn't leave Dario's side. She handed him the bottle and sat down on one of his chairs.

"I locked up," she told him, and he sighed gratefully. Of course, if there was an emergency, he would help, but hopefully there would be no more sick or injured animals walking through his door today.

"Gracias," he told his sister, taking a long swig of the beer.

"That was brutal," she said, kicking her feet up onto his desk.

"Thanks for sticking around," he replied.

"Any time, baby brother," she crossed her ankles. "So, what took you so long to get back?" she asked.

Dario felt a flush creep along his cheeks, but he shrugged one noncommittal shoulder up. "Lost track of time," he said, as casually as possible.

Tamya narrowed her eyes at him. "Mmmhmm," she responded, not sounding convinced.

As she opened her mouth, likely to press the issue further, a knock sounded at the door. Both Dario and Tamya groaned in unison.

"I'll go," his sister grumbled, but Dario stood up first.

"No, I'll go. You've done enough today," he said, patting her on the shoulder as he walked out.

Dario placed his beer on the welcome counter, then crossed the room to unlock the door. He swung it open, then froze.

It was Asiri.

Asiri was standing right in front of him, but she looked completely different.

Gone was the dark, simple clothing she usually wore. Gone were the oversized tunics and black trousers. Instead, she was wearing a shirt the color of the sky over the sea, a full pollera with some pretty flowers, and a brightly patterned wrap. Dario dragged his gaze back up to her face and found her smiling at him nervously.

"Hola," she said softly.

"Hola," he replied dumbly, looking back down at her new outfit. "You look ..." his voice trailed off, and she smiled a little shyly.

"I look?" she prompted, when suddenly Tamya burst out of the backroom.

"Who is it Dario, is it urgent or can we go home?" Then she noticed Asiri. "Oh, hello! Nice skirt."

Asiri looked from Tamya to Dario, then Tamya again, the smile melting from her face. Finally, she bit her lip and looked at the ground.

"You're with someone. I'm sorry, I should have ..." she wouldn't meet his eyes. What had happened? What had he done? "I'll go," she finished, spinning around.

Dario shot a desperate look at Tamya, and his sister understood immediately.

"No, please don't go!" she called after Asiri. "I was just leaving my brother here to finish locking up by himself. My girlfriend must be wondering where I am, anyway," she finished, grabbing both her bag and the sleeping guinea pig. "I'll take Pepe tonight," she said, squeezing by Dario. Gently, she guided Asiri inside. "See you mañana, hermano!" Then she was gone.

They were quiet for a moment, Asiri twisting the tie of her shawl, while Dario stood there, arms at his sides, unsure of what to say. He was afraid of spooking her again.

"So ..." Asiri started. "Sister?"

Dario finally understood. Thank the dioses Tamya was more perceptive than he was!

"Si, si, Tamya is my sister!" he told her quickly. "She sometimes comes to help with the animals. It was sort of a busy day today. There were so many patients brought in, she was nice enough to stay to help."

"Oh," was all she responded, but Dario thought she looked pleased.

"Do you want to come in? I have some cerveza in the back," he asked her.

Asiri hesitated. "Are a lot of your patients still here?" she asked.

Dario nodded. "Quite a few today, actually. Including a very cute chimú dog that I'm planning on adopting if no one claims her. She's great."

Asiri smiled at him, and Dario's mouth went dry.

"Do you ... do you want to meet her?" he asked her. She liked dogs, right? Almost everyone liked dogs, didn't they?

Asiri hesitated, but then gave a small nod. "I'd love to meet her."

Dario held out his hand, and she took it immediately, sending tickles of electricity through his arm. Dario led her to his office slowly to preserve the sensation, then opened the door.

The pup immediately went to launch herself at him, but when she saw Asiri, she changed directions entirely and reached up to plant her big paws on Asiri's stomach.

Right over her clean, new shirt, Dario realized a second too late. He lunged to stop her, but the dog was already jumping up and down, licking at any exposed skin Asiri might have. Not that Dario could blame her. He wanted to do the exact same thing. Unfortunately, she was mussing and crinkling Asiri's clothing in the process.

"I'm so sorry, ah carajo, I'm sorry!" he told her, cringing, still futilely trying to pry the dog away from her. To his complete astonishment, Asiri threw back her head and laughed.

Dario was struck by it, and by her, her chin tilted back to expose the elegant column of her neck. Her lips parted and her eyes crinkled at the corners.

"Don't be sorry," Asiri said. "She's as lovely as you said." And then Asiri, in all her pretty new clothes, sat right down on the floor to play with the puppy.

And Dario fell head over heels in love.

JACAMAR

CHAPTER 23

ASIRI

"Hi! Hi!" the puppy yipped in a deliriously happy tone. "Friend? New friend? Hi, good girl! Hi, sweet girl!"

Asiri couldn't help but laugh. It was clear that the dog had learned those phrases from someone, and she had a pretty good guess at who that was.

"Hola amiga," she crooned, petting her head and scratching behind her ears. Her tail wagged so hard it looked like a gray blur. "What brought you here, preciosa?"

"I found her by the playa, severely overheated and dehydrated," Dario explained, sinking to sit next to her on the floor. "She wasn't doing well at all, poor girl, but she's getting better every day."

"Dario saved me!" the puppy told her, butt now wagging as well with the force of her tail. "Good boy, strong boy! He saved me and now I have food and water and playtime!" She launched herself at Dario and licked him several times under the chin while Dario tried to calm her down. "I have a home!"

Asiri's heart sank a little with worry. "Does she belong to anyone?" she asked Dario quietly.

"I belong to Dario! He's a good boy," the puppy responded.

"No one has come to claim her yet," Dario told her.

"What will you do ..." she didn't want to finish the sentence, but Dario understood her.

"If no one comes, I'm taking her home with me," he replied, and Asiri could hear the pleasure in his voice at the prospect. Her chest eased with relief.

"Do you have a name picked out?" she asked him, and Dario looked down at the ground sheepishly.

"I shouldn't ..." he mumbled, and Asiri grinned.

"But you do," she guessed.

He shrugged. "Maybe."

"Well? What is it?" she insisted.

"I don't want to get my hopes up," he replied.

Asiri's lips twisted as she tried to suppress a grin. "But you already have a name, at least in your mind."

Dario's heart shone through his eyes as the puppy settled into his lap, letting out a loud, contented sigh.

"Choclo," he finally answered.

"Choclo?" Asiri burst out laughing. Dario shrugged.

"She's like an ear of corn, with a little tuft of hair on her head," he explained.

"Choclo," Asiri repeated. "I like it."

Choclo began blinking slowly, fatigue settling over her like a blanket. Her eyes became hooded, her muscles relaxed, and her tail began a steady swish, swish, swish over the floor.

Then, the dog began to sing softly.

"In the mountain fields, you will run.

You will jump, over rocks and stones.

You will lay, in the soft sun.

And wake again, to bury your bones."

"Que lindo," Asiri murmured to her as she smoothed her hand over her back, and Choclo's tail moved faster.

"Dario sang it to me every night when I was sick," the puppy told her, nuzzling into Dario's lap. Asiri watched as Choclo gazed up at him with complete adoration, and she was afraid that she might be looking at the man with the exact same expression. Then Choclo shut her eyes with a soft sigh.

She and Dario stared at each other over Choclo's sleeping form, and Asiri's breath caught in her throat. She had almost forgotten the reason she was there. Nervously, she twisted one of her braids in her fingers.

"I wanted—" she started,

"Have you—" Dario said at the same time. They both stopped and exchanged shy smiles.

"Go ahead," Asiri urged. "What were you going to say?"

"I was just wondering if you had eaten yet. I mean, I know you probably have. It's already late, far past dinner time. And Julio's bar will be closed, but maybe you ate there earlier, or had something at home. I just asked because when we got back from the waterfall ..." his eyes dipped to the ground and Asiri flushed, realizing he was remembering what had happened behind the falls. "Well, it was just a really busy day, and I had a lot of patients, and I didn't get a chance to eat, but I was going to go make myself something at home now," he finished in a rush.

Asiri blinked at him. It was more than she had ever heard him say in one go.

Dario took a deep breath. "So, would you like to?"

Asiri's brows furrowed. "Would I like to what?"

Dario's face scrunched up, and it looked like he was counting. After a few moments, he opened his eyes and regarded her more calmly. "If you haven't already eaten, would you like to come to my house for a meal?" he asked, his words slow and deliberate.

Asiri, for once, didn't hesitate. "I'd love to," she confessed.

Dario's look of relief as he helped her off the floor only solidified her decision, and as they walked out the front door, she didn't let go of his hand.

Asiri wasn't sure what to expect of Dario's home. Something modest, perhaps; small but comfortable, filled with books and cages and animal fur.

She wasn't far off with the animal fur. There was definitely some dog and cat (and possibly other animal) hair here in there, but the space was far more clean and organized than she had expected. The outside of his house was straight out of a fairytale, with happy flower planters at the windows, pretty teal shutters, and a wide double door that opened into a small courtyard. He'd decorated the rest of his home with bright tapestries, the majority depicting different animals or nature scenes, embroidered pillows, and colorful throws. There were a few dirty dishes in a water basin, but other than that, the kitchen was also clean and well organized, and better stocked than she had expected for a bachelor.

Dario had her sit on a tall stool at the kitchen counter, whipping up a quick Pisco Sour and adamantly refusing her help with cooking.[1] She sipped on the citrusy drink as he chopped, marinated, sautéed, and roasted. In the end, his quick recipe of arroz con pollo was ready by the time she had finished her first drink, and he deftly placed a second at the table, along with one of his own, as he set it.

Dario pulled out her chair as they sat to eat, and her heart kicked up in her chest as his fingers grazed the backs of her shoulders. Trying to tamp down her wave of lust, Asiri picked up her fork and took a bite. As the flavors hit her tongue, she couldn't help but let out a soft moan. The rice was light and fluffy, perfectly seasoned with garlic and cilantro. The chicken was slightly crispy on the outside and perfectly cooked within. The simple vegetables roasted in butter added a little sweetness to the dish. All in all, it was one of the best meals Asiri had ever had.

Though she would concede that the company might have had something to do with it.

As they ate, Asiri told Dario about Doña Iris's afternoon lessons, and how weaving and cloth making were a lot harder than she had anticipated.

"But afterward, Doña Iris told me that I have been doing very well," Asiri told him with a blush. Then she ran a hand over her skirt. "She gifted me these new clothes. I have never had anything so pretty. When I put them on and saw myself, all I could think of was that I wanted you to see me in them too," she admitted softly, her blush deepening.

---

1. A Pisco Sour is a traditional Peruvian drink made from Pisco (a liquor made from grapes) lime juice, sugar, an egg white to create a frothy foam, and topped with amargo bitters.

Dario was quiet long enough that Asiri began to regret her decision to be honest with him. She felt foolish and vulnerable, and suddenly wished she hadn't said anything at all. In fact, she wished she hadn't had the crazy impulse to find him in his practice in the first place. She should have stayed home, had dinner with Paloma at Julio's Tavern and gone to bed early. This was silly. *She* was being silly. Just because they had shared a moment of intimacy at the lake didn't mean that Dario was looking for anything more. She was about to push back from the table and stand to leave when Dario reached out to grab her hand. Looking in her eyes, Dario lifted it and pressed a kiss to the center of her palm.

"Te ves bella," he murmured, shifting to kiss the inside of her wrist. "The clothes are beautiful, but you make them radiant." His lips reached the crook of her elbow. "I haven't stopped thinking about you all day," he told her in a voice that made heat rush between her legs.

"I haven't stopped thinking about you either," she whispered.

His hand found her leg underneath the table, and he gripped the back of her calf right below her knee. Then, with a quick, strong pull, he dragged her forward, trapping her between his splayed thighs. Instinctively, she gripped at his shoulders, her fingers bunching the fabric underneath her grasp.

They leaned in at the same time, mouths brushing in the softest of kisses. It wasn't like the fast, heady desperation that drove them behind the falls. This was different, this was unhurried. They were not moving simply because of their body's desires; there was deliberation behind it. They had made a choice.

Asiri's lips parted with a sigh and she felt Dario's tongue brush against her own, still tasting like lime. She sucked it into her mouth and felt his grip tighten around her waist. Dario stood up, slowly, lifting her with him, and began backing her towards his bedroom, his mouth never breaking contact with hers. As they stood in the threshold of his doorway, he leaned her back against the archway, moving to kiss behind her ear and down to her shoulder.

Asiri grasped the bottom of his shirt and lifted it over his head, allowing herself to move her fingers over the tight muscles of his abdomen, which trembled underneath her touch. His mouth paused its slow perusal of her skin to breathe heavily against her neck as she traveled over all the defined ridges of his torso and traced the light dusting of hair over his skin. When her fingers found his nipples, he pressed against her, moving his hands over her breasts, as if he wanted to mirror her motions.

Asiri only allowed him to remove her shirt and skirt before stopping him. Earlier at the falls, he had distracted her so thoroughly she hadn't had a chance to explore him the way that she had wanted to. She wasn't going to let him distract her again.

Deliberately, she pushed him towards the bed, undoing his belt as he walked backwards. When it was free, she slowly slid her hands inside his pants and undergarments, sinking to the floor as she pushed all the fabric off of him. Then she gazed up at his naked body, reveling in the sight of him all lean and long and hard above her.

"Asiri," he groaned, cupping the back of her head and trying to pull her up to him, but she resisted. Instead, she placed hot, open-mouthed kisses on his thick legs, moving closer and closer to the insides of his thighs. He groaned again, a little bit more helplessly, and the hand at her head clenched around her hair.

"Sorry," he murmured, instantly loosening his grip, but Asiri hadn't minded it. In fact, seeing him like this, on the brink of desperation, made her feel powerful and wanted. She shifted up on her knees and took a long, slow lick of his cock, swirling her tongue around the tip of him.

His head jerked backwards and his entire body shuddered.

"Asiri," he repeated, his voice gravelly. She licked him again, this time pulling him into her mouth when she reached the tip, and sucking. Her head bobbed up and down as she got accustomed to his girth, wetness pooling between her legs as his moans and praise filled her ears, as his thick hardness filled her mouth. Now she understood how Dario had finished just by tasting her. She didn't think it would take much to send her over the edge right now, either.

Abruptly, Dario pulled her away from him and lifted her up completely, her legs instinctively wrapping around his waist. Twisting, he brought them both down on the bed, and the feeling of him completely on top of her made her vision erupt in tiny specks of light.

Dario wasted no time in removing her final layers, and then they were naked. Hot skin to skin, aching flesh against flesh. He kissed her deeply, moving himself over her, the moisture between her legs making his cock rub effortlessly over her swollen clit.

Then his mouth was on her breasts, his tongue tracing a pattern down to her stomach, briefly dipping into her navel before continuing. She thought he would take her in his mouth again, but to her surprise, when he got down to her legs, he gripped them tightly and flipped her over onto her belly. A shocked gasp escaped her, but then his mouth was back on her, kissing the inside of her ankle, licking up her calf, leaving small, delicious bites up and down her thighs. Her hands reached up to grip his bedsheets, the thrill of not knowing where his hands and fingers and mouth would land next, both exhilarating and tormenting.

Then he was palming her ass, his finger moving down to slide through her slick wetness. She arched back against him and moaned.

"Por favor, Dario," she begged, as his fingers circled her entrance languidly. He slid up, covering more of her body with his. His fingers found her clit, then moved to trace more maddening circles as she whimpered. He kissed the valley at the center of her back and ghosted his mouth over her ribs.

"You are the most beautiful thing I've ever seen," he whispered to her, finally slipping a finger inside of her. She nearly sobbed with relief. "I feel you all day, inside of me. Inside of my head, imprinted on the backs of my lids when I close my eyes."

Another finger slid in.

"I feel you just below the surface of my skin, as if all I would have to do is scratch deep enough to draw you out of me," he continued.

One more finger, and Asiri bit the pillow to keep from screaming.

"But why would I ever want to be rid of you?" His fingers began moving, pumping slowly, in and out of her. "I want to drive you in, deeper still. Only when you reach the very center of me, only when my heart can beat you through my very veins, only then will it be enough."

His fingers moved faster and harder, and Asiri reached around to grip his hair in her hand. She pulled him towards her, twisting her neck to kiss him, sloppy and uncoordinated, but full of every emotion that was flooding her chest.

Dario slipped himself out of her and flipped her over once more. He stared at her face, sweat dotting his temple, his hair wild and mussed. Asiri reached down and gripped him in her hand, pumping him languidly, deliberately, all while pulling him closer to her.

"Please," she whispered. "I want you deeper inside of me, too."

At her confession, Dario framed Asiri's face within his palms, and in one fluid motion, sheathed himself fully in her wet heat.

They both moaned in unison, Asiri's legs tensing and gripping him closer to her. He looked deep into her eyes, then kissed her delicately before beginning to move.

His strokes were slow and steady, but he kept his body close to hers, his pelvis rubbing against where she needed it most with every thrust. She moved with him, arching her hips in tandem, her hands roving over his back, his ass, his arms, his face. It was as if she could not touch him enough, could not be close enough to him. Then he began moving faster, building Asiri's pleasure. It rose higher and higher, taking on a more jagged edge until she was whimpering and clawing at his shoulders, desperate for him to give her more.

The muscles in Dario's arms bunched as he lifted his torso, bracing himself over her, his hips driving harder into her. Asiri moaned and arched her back, almost delirious with pleasure. Then, using a strength she didn't know was possible, Dario shifted his weight to a single hand, while his other snaked in between their bodies to stroke her. The combination of feeling him inside of her while also pleasuring her with his fingers was too much, and she shattered, her body shaking as she let out a low, guttural moan. With a few more thrusts, Dario joined her, leaning forward to capture her mouth in one last gasping kiss.

HONEY BEAR / KINKAJOU

CHAPTER 24

DARIO

D ario rolled to his side, pulling Asiri into his arms as he did so. They lay there entwined together for a long moment until he could feel both their hearts slow to a normal rhythm. After a while she moved back slightly, enough to look him in the eye.

With a satisfied smile, he pushed her hair away from her face.

"Hola," he said.

"Hola," she replied softly.

Dario took a moment to look at her, cheeks still flushed, hair wild, lips plump and swollen. He let his hand roam over her bare skin, marveling at the rises and falls of her body, where hard muscle turned into pliant flesh and then back again.

"How are you? Do you need anything?" he asked. "Agua?"

She shook her head and felt her hair tickling his shoulder.

"No, just, el baño?" she asked. He pointed to a door behind her and she stood, robbing him of her heat. He couldn't mind too much, as he could admire all of her lovely bare skin before she disappeared behind the door.

While she was gone, he filled two glasses up with water any-way—just in case—and turned down the bed so that he could easily cover them with the blankets should she get cold. He was really hoping that she was planning on spending the night.

When she emerged, he did his best not to gawk at her, but he couldn't believe he was so lucky. Even luckier when she slid back into his bed and immediately returned to his arms. He held her, resting his head on her hair.

"I think I'll bring the Amaru extra fish tomorrow," Dario said drowsily.

"Why?" Asiri asked.

"He's the reason you and I got to spend so much time together. I think he's owed a thanks," Dario replied.

Asiri laughed, and Dario admired the long column of her throat. Then he looped his finger gently around the golden chain decorating it, tracing his fingers down to the pendant which hung between her breasts.

"What's this?" he asked her.

Asiri wrapped her hand around his, but didn't move it away from her necklace.

"It was my mother's," she responded with a sweet smile. "I never really knew her. She died when I was just a baby. This is all that I have of hers."

"Does your father still live?" he asked, and immediately wished he hadn't as a dark look crossed her face. At first, he didn't think that she would respond.

"He does," she finally said. "But he isn't a very kind person. One of the reasons I moved to Pisqu was to get away from him."

Fury and fear flooded Dario's system, and his hand instinctively gripped her chain tighter. "Did he hurt you?" he asked, his voice low.

Thankfully, Asiri shook her head. "No, not like that, in any case. He just didn't care about me. He cared about what I could do for him, but in the end, I don't think he ever really knew me." She looked down at their clasped hands above her chest. "But at least he let me keep this one piece of my mother."

"It's beautiful," he answered, touched that she would share so much of herself with him. "I don't mean to speak ill of your family, but I don't think I like your father very much.

Amusement flickered across her face. "No?" she asked.

Dario shook his head. "Not if he didn't make you feel cared for."

Asiri shrugged. "After my mother died... I don't know if he was capable of loving again."

"I can't imagine anyone meeting you and not loving you."

The words were out of his mouth before he could think about them, and their implication. Asiri jerked her head up in surprise. Dario's heart clenched in his chest and panic raced through his veins. Had he said too much? Was it too soon? Would she pull away again? Would she leave? He began to feel short of breath and dizzy; the room began to spin. No, not spin. The room began to shake with the intensity of his worry. Then Asiri gripped his arm, jolting up in bed.

"Dario," she gasped, her voice full of concern. It was then he noticed that the room actually *was* shaking, picture frames were rocking back and forth on the walls, and the furniture was rumbling and vibrating.

It was an earthquake.

Dario leapt out of bed, pulling Asiri along with him. He placed them both underneath the curved arch of his bedroom doorway, naked and vulnerable. Dario braced his arms against the frame, shielding Asiri with as much of his own body as possible. Somewhere, something crashed on the floor and he felt Asiri flinch, burying her head into his chest.

After what seemed like an eternity, the shaking finally tapered, and then stopped altogether. He let go of the wood, wincing as his hands cramped from the force of his grip. He flexed his fingers a few times, willing the rest of his muscles to relax.

Dario could not remember being more frightened in his entire life. Their country was no stranger to earthquakes, and Pisqu had seen their fair share of them, but he only ever worried about himself before now. But having Asiri with him changed everything. He would have cracked himself open and tucked her inside his ribcage if he knew it would keep her safe.

"How are you?" he asked her, a little breathless. He cupped her face in his hands. "Are you hurt?" his gaze roved over her body.

"I'm fine," she told him shakily. "Are you all right?" her fingers gripped his wrists.

Slowly, he lowered his forehead to hers and released a long breath.

"I am now," he told her.

Reluctantly, Dario pulled away from Asiri and began gathering his clothing. "I need to check on the patients at the clinic," he told her. "Will you come with me? I don't want to leave you here alone."

"Of course," Asiri said, already putting her own clothes back on. Dario sighed in relief. He wanted her close to him, in case another earthquake were to hit. But just as Asiri had finished putting on her shoes, her body jerked backwards and she hit his dresser, crying out in pain.

"Asiri! Asiri!" he cried, catching her in his arms as she stumbled. She shook, one of her hands pressed against her forehead.

"The Amaru," she muttered, her voice barely audible.

"Que?" Dario asked, confused. "Asiri, please, what's the matter?"

With a gulp of air, Asiri's eyes flew open. She looked at him desperately.

"The Amaru," she gasped. "We need to get to the Amaru."

A little while later, he and Asiri were scrambling through the forest, the first orange-blush rays of sunrise peeking over the horizon.

"I don't understand," he said for what felt like the hundredth time. "How do you know that the Amaru needs help?"

Asiri didn't answer, just kept pulling him through the woods.

"Asiri, stop," he demanded, pulling her back. She glared at him furiously.

"Please," he begged. "Talk to me. What just happened?"

Dario watched as her jaw clenched so hard, he could almost hear her teeth grinding. Her eyes were pleading, but he couldn't just continue to follow her blindly. "What is going on?" he asked again, as gently as he could.

"The Amaru," Asiri started, then bit her lip. With a frustrated groan, she closed her eyes. When she opened them again, she looked more resolved.

"The Amaru sent me a message," she said. "He spoke to me. He said I needed to come now. So we need to hurry," she stressed, trying to pull him forward.

"The Amaru?" Dario repeated. "It spoke to you?"

"Yes," Asiri replied.

"Just now? After the earthquake?"

Asiri was silent.

"Asiri?"

"Before the earthquake, too. I have been able to understand him since we first found him. He speaks to me, and I can understand him," she confessed in a rush.

Dario's mouth fell open. "How? If he can communicate, why haven't I heard him too?"

Dario watched as Asiri's face fell, looking lost. Then she squared her shoulders with resolve.

"Because I can speak to animals. I am a Creature Communer. I can communicate with them. I've been able to since I was a child."

Dario's head spun harder than it had with the earthquake.

"Que?" was all he was able to say.

"I come from a place in the Andes. It's called Casa de Murmuros. It's a house for people with special abilities, like me. I loved it at first, I really did. It was home. But through the years, I began feeling more and more like my gift was being abused by my father, the shaman. He heads the house. It's why I left, why I moved to Pisqu. I didn't want to be used anymore. I wanted to live my own life," Asiri's words were fast and frantic, and Dario could barely make sense of them.

"You ... you can speak to animals?" he asked her.

Asiri let out a grunt of frustration. "Yes," she stressed. "And the Amaru is in trouble. We need to go."

She can speak to animals? Dario wondered. It wasn't as if he didn't believe her— he didn't *not* believe her— it was just such a fantastical thought. No one could speak to animals, right? That ability didn't exist.

You weren't really sure that Amarus existed either, a voice inside his head said.

"You don't believe me," Asiri said, her shoulders slumping.

"It's not that ..." Dario started, unsure of how to word his thoughts and feelings. It was all a lot.

"I can prove it to you," Asiri said, determinedly. "Choclo told me that you sang her a song every day when she was still very sick. A song about running in the mountain fields."

"With plenty of bones to hide away," Dario finished for her. He blew out a strong breath through his teeth. No one knew about that song. It was one that he had made up. He would sing it to Choclo only after locking up for the night, when it was hard for the pup to sleep because of her injuries. There was no way Asiri could have known about the song. The only ones who had ever heard it were him ... and Choclo.

"All right," Dario declared. It was crazy and wild and outlandish, but he believed her. Asiri could speak to animals. "I believe you," he said.

Asiri's face erupted with pure relief, and this time, when she pulled him deeper into the forest, he followed.

YELLOW SPOTTED RIVER TURTLE / TARICAYA

CHAPTER 25

ASIRI

When Asiri and Dario reached the Amaru, he had already half-dragged his body out of the cave and was agitatedly rocking his snakelike body. As soon as they were in his sight, he grunted, and stabbing pain assaulted Asiri's head once more. She doubled over in pain.

Come! the Amaru yelled inside her mind. *Come!*

"We're here!" she cried out, swallowing down a wave of nausea that hit her at the power within his voice.

Terremoto, the Amaru said, softer this time.

"Yes, we know there was an earthquake," Asiri answered. "We felt it. Are you hurt?"

Terremoto! the Amaru insisted more urgently. *Playa, take me to playa.*

Asiri turned to Dario in confusion. "He's telling us to take him to the beach," she told him.

Dario's brows pulled down. "The beach? Now? Why?"

"Why?" Asiri repeated to the Amaru.

Terremoto, it said again.

"He just keeps repeating 'earthquake,'" she answered hopelessly.

"We felt the earthquake," Dario told the Amaru, placing his hand over the creature's head comfortingly. "We know, you're safe now."

PLAYA, his voice boomed in Asiri's skull, and she fell to her knees. *PLAYA,* it repeated, and her hands flew to the sides of her head, pressing down as if to keep it from cracking open. *PLAYA!*

"Beach, beach," she repeated, tears streaming down her face. Dario was there on the ground with her, his arms wrapped around her body, doing his best to shield her from the Amaru.

"Stop!" he yelled at it. "Stop it, you're hurting her!"

PLAYA! PLAYA!

Asiri cried, trembling in Dario's arms.

"Fine! We'll take you! We'll take you to the shore!" Dario yelled at the creature, and suddenly all the pain and pressure in Asiri's head stopped. She stayed in Dario's embrace as her breathing evened out, feeling him rock her gently. Finally, she pulled back, wiping her face with her new blue blouse, and met Dario's worried eyes. He lifted his hands to her cheeks, rubbing underneath her eyes with her thumbs.

"I'm all right," she told him, her voice hoarse. Had she been screaming? "I'm all right," she repeated, struggling to her feet.

Dario made sure she was steady before whirling on the Amaru. "Damn you," he growled at the creature. "I don't care that you're a semidios, I don't care that you are the stuff of legends. I don't even care if you curse me, but damn you for hurting her."

Asiri placed a hand on his arm. "It's all right now," she said as calmly as possible. "Let's just get him there."

Dario and Asiri grabbed the Amaru and began carrying him toward the shore. It was a much longer walk than when they had moved the Amaru from the river to the cave, and they were both quickly drenched in sweat. By the time they were close to Pisqu, the sun had fully ascended into the sky. As they made their way to the beach, Asiri heard her name being called.

"Asiri! Asiri!" someone yelled. Turning her head, she could see that it was Paloma, running to her, Paqari not far behind.

"Coño, mujer!" Paqari growled as he chased after her.

"Asiri, are you all right? I couldn't find you at your house, so I went to Dario's clinic, but you weren't there either—*what is that?*"

The last part of Paloma's sentence came out as a screech, and she backed up into Paqari's chest. The man didn't attempt to remove her, instead he placed a protective hand on one of her shoulders.

"Is that ... Asiri, is that ..." Paloma stammered.

"It's an Amaru," Dario replied, still moving towards the ocean. "It's a long story, but we need to get it to the beach."

"That thing will curse us all," Paqari said darkly.

"No, it won't," Asiri insisted, and found she still believed it. Even though her head still throbbed from the Amaru's assault, she was fairly certain that he hadn't meant to hurt her. His tone had been full of anxious desperation, not malice.

"I don't understand," Paloma said, staring at the Amaru like it was about to leap out of their arms and eat them all.

"Please, just trust me," Asiri grunted, straining under the weight of the semidios.

After a moment's hesitation, Paloma ran up and placed her hands under the Amaru, bearing some of its weight.

"I trust you," she told Asiri, who felt prickles behind her eyes. She beamed at her friend.

"Coño, carajo!" Paqari swore, then crossed over to the three of them to lend his strength as well. "If this thing curses me, I'm kicking your ass," he told Dario.

Together they made their way to the shore, placing the injured Amaru on the warm sand.

Terremoto, the Amaru said to Asiri, gentler but still insistent. She frowned at his words.

"What did he say?" Dario asked her.

"What do you mean, 'what did he say?'" Paqari demanded.

"He just keeps repeating, 'earthquake,'"Asiri answered.

"You can understand him?" Paloma gaped at her.

"All animals, actually," she told her friend nervously. Paloma stared at her, her mouth comically agape. Then her lips stretched into a small grin.

"You have a gift too," she said, and Asiri nodded.

"You can't seriously expect me to believe—" Paqari started, but before he could finish, they were all knocked from their feet. The world began shaking again, sand dunes shifting and tumbling, the ocean's waves erratic and frantic. Dario rolled to cover Asiri's body with his, and from the corner of her eye she could see Paqari doing the same for Paloma. It lasted longer this time, and they could hear the screams of the townspeople from the village behind them. Asiri worried that the ground was going to crack open and swallow them whole. Then, everything stopped. The four of them stared at each other for a long moment, wondering if the danger was finally over.

That question was answered when suddenly, the ocean disappeared.

"What?" Paqari mumbled, scrambling to his feet, watching as all the water was sucked backwards, farther than the eye could see, leaving only the ocean floor in its wake. Asiri looked at Dario, confused, and saw his face had gone completely white.

"Que?" Asiri began, when in the distance, the largest wave she had ever seen began rushing into view. It was enormous, taller than even the highest trees in the Andes, stretching towards the skyline and towering over everything. Asiri could only watch, horror filling her chest as it barreled its way towards them. It would destroy the entire town.

It would destroy everything.

Dario pulled her into a tight embrace, angling her away from the imminent destruction. "Don't look," she heard him whisper against her ear, and she squeezed her eyes shut, throwing her arms around him and holding on as tightly as she could, glad that if she was going to die, at least it would be in his arms.

"Wait, look!" she heard Paloma cry out, and she shifted around just in time to see the Amaru stretch his wings and break through all his bindings. His injured wing still looked painful, dotted with missing feathers and angry red welts, the bone jutting at an awkward angle. But it stretched them wide and flapped, whirling sand all around them as he beat his wings, lifting himself up into the sky.

Asiri watched in amazement as the Amaru flew askew towards the monstrous wave, his snout low and set, eyes firm and determined. She cried out when it seemed as if the wave was going to collide into him, but right before it connected, an enormous burst of light shot out from the Amaru, extending up just as high as the top of the wave, but as far out on either side of him as Asiri could see. When the wave struck, it halted in its path, water smacking into and sloshing over the barrier of light. The Amaru shuddered in the air, wings and body tensing as if under an enormous strain. Finally, the sea receded, slowly falling back to its normal level, and there was an eruption of cheers behind them.

Asiri spun around to see that they had gathered a large crowd. Townspeople who had clearly been terrified were wiping away tears and hugging their loved ones. The threat was over. Asiri looked at Dario with a wobbly smile, wanting to share her relief, but to her surprise, he wasn't looking at her.

"No," he said, so quietly she almost missed it. Then he broke away from her and began running towards the water. Only then did Asiri notice the Amaru, head slumped and wings beating slower and slower. His body was approaching the ground too fast and suddenly he stopped trying to fly altogether, plummeting towards the ground.

"No!" she cried out, chasing after Dario. He reached the Amaru moments after his limp form crashed into the surf, Asiri a few steps behind him. Together, they dragged the Amaru away from the sea and back onto the sand.

"Will he be all right?" Paloma asked behind them.

"Yes," Asiri answered quickly, then jerked her head towards Dario when he didn't respond. "Dario, he'll be all right, won't he?"

Dario looked at her helplessly, the Amaru's llama head cradled in his lap. "Asiri, I—"

"No!" Asiri snapped, running her hands over the creature's body. "No, he will be fine!"

"Asiri," Dario repeated softly.

"He saved us! He saved us all, Dario!" Asiri yelled, feeling hot, wet tears on her cheeks.

"I know, amor," was all he said.

Asiri leaned in close to the Amaru, her lips inches from his ear. "Please," she whispered. "Please come back to us."

She had almost given up when a vision flickered through her mind. Asiri gasped and squeezed her eyes closed, trying to get a clearer picture. She saw the Amaru—no, wait—she saw part of the Amaru. It was his spirit form, but it wasn't complete. Instead of his wings and llama head, he was instead fully serpent, save for his fish's tail. He was lying on some dark stones, fog all around him. He looked lost, swiveling his little snake head from side to side. In the distance, she saw shadow figures approaching him.

Then, another vision, the Amaru again, but this time he was fully llama. His spirit form was on a beach, wandering on the surf, and Asiri could see the blurry forms of people behind him.

Finally, the Amaru again, this time in condor form, floating aimlessly through the dark space, glittering starlight surrounding him.

Asiri reared back with a gasp.

"I know what I have to do," she said.

SLOTH / PEREZOSO

Chapter 26

Asiri

"His spirit is fragmented," Asiri explained to Dario, Paloma, and Paqari as they all carried the Amaru towards Dario's clinic. "His serpent form is in Ukhu Pacha, his llama form is here in Kay Pacha, and his condor form is in Hanan Pacha."

"So he's gone?" Paloma asked, voice wobbly. Asiri shook her head.

"No, he's not gone. Because I am going to go get him," she responded firmly.

"Coño," Paqari muttered.

"Is that all you say?" Paloma snapped at him.

"What do you mean, you're 'going to go get him?'" Dario asked as they reached the clinic.

"Dario!" someone called out. They all turned their heads to see Tamya running towards them, with the guinea pig in his sling.

"What happened?" she asked. "After the first earthquake I came here, I thought you would come to check on the animals. But then people said you were at the beach and—*is that an Amaru?*"

"I'll explain, but we need to get him inside," Dario grunted, shifting the Amaru's sizable weight. Tamya dashed in front of them to unlock the clinic. As they moved to transport the creature inside, a hummingbird zoomed out from the town center and perched on Asiri's shoulder.

"Asiri! Are you all right? That was a big earthquake!" Felipe chirped in her ear.

"I'm fine, my friend, but the Amaru isn't. I need to help him," Asiri responded.

"Did she just speak to that hummingbird?" Tamya asked in an incredulous voice.

"Later," Dario responded.

Together they lifted the Amaru onto a large table, and Asiri faced the group.

"I have visited the pachas before," she explained. "It was, well, it was sort of part of my job back where I'm from. I can go there and unite his spirit forms, so that he can come back to his earthly body."

"You want to visit the underworld?" Paloma screeched.

Asiri shrugged. "It's not that bad, really. It's where many of our dead reside, after all, and the dioses wouldn't make all of that land terrible. And Pachamama is there, remember?" she said, referring to the great earth mother.

"The supay are also there," Dario reminded her, with a frown. "Asiri, I don't like this. I know that your father was a shaman, and that you have a gift, but this is too dangerous." His voice dropped, and he took her hand. "I don't want to lose you."

She squeezed his fingers with as much reassurance as she could. "You won't. I've done this before. Besides, he saved us. All of us. He saved the entire town," she reminded him, gesturing to the motionless Amaru.

"Debts should be paid," Paqari agreed gruffly, surprising her.

Felipe sprung from Asiri's shoulder and flitted in front of her face, dashing back and forth so quickly her eyes struggled to keep up with his form.

"You can't go alone, Asiri!" he said, voice worried. "You need guides! It's too dangerous!"

Asiri shook her head. "There is no time, Felipe!"

"What is he saying?" Paloma asked.

"So she *is* talking to the colibrí?" Tamya asked, but they all ignored her.

"Nothing, he's just worried," Asiri answered quickly.

"Asiri, what aren't you telling us?" Dario demanded. She opened her mouth to set him at ease, but Paloma whirled around to glare at her.

"Don't you dare lie to us," she commanded in a tone that bore no argument, and Asiri's shoulders slumped.

"I know. She got me with that one too," she heard Paqari grumble. "Might as well tell us, she'll get it out of you one way or another."

Asiri sighed.

"I usually visit the pachas with guides," she confessed. "A snake to guide me through Ukhu Pacha. A cougar for Kay Pacha, and a condor for Hanan Pacha."

"The sacred three," Dario said, realization lighting his features. Asiri nodded.

"But there's no time! There are no cougars near the coast, and even the condors don't always come out this way. And every minute we stand here arguing, he's slipping away!" she cried out, pointing back to the Amaru.

"I'll take you Asiri!" Felipe chirped.

"No, my friend, you're too small," Asiri answered, though she was deeply touched. Shock crossed Dario's face as the hummingbird perched on his shoulder, if only to ruffle out his feathers and glare at Asiri.

"I am a creature of the skies," he reminded her, his voice haughty. "I may not be a sacred condor, but I have wings, and I am welcome in Hanan Pacha."

Dario looked at Asiri for translation.

"He says he will be my animal guide in Hanan Pacha," she said softly, throat getting thick with emotion.

"And I will lead you in Kay Pacha," a rough voice boomed. Asiri jumped and looked at Tamya.

"What?" Dario's sister said, looking nervous. Asiri looked down at the sling she carried. In all the commotion, she forgot that Tamya was carrying Marco.

"*You* will guide me?" Asiri asked him, shocked.

"I said I would, didn't I? Stupid humans, never good at listening," the guinea pig grumbled.

Asiri looked up at Dario with wide eyes. "He says he'll join me in Kay Pacha," she told him.

"He? Who?" Dario asked, turning towards Tamya. Then realization crossed his face. "Pepe?"

"My name is not Pepe—"

"His name is not Pepe," Asiri interrupted. "It's Marco. Marco Ignacio Lorenzo Gonzales Palacios de la Cruz."

For once, the cuy was stunned silent.

"That's …" Dario faltered. "That's a lot for a guinea pig."

Asiri shrugged, then turned back to Marco. "Why?" she asked him. "Why would you want to help me? You don't even like me!"

"He doesn't?" Dario asked, surprised. Asiri ignored him.

"For the Amaru, of course. Can't have our semidioses dying. And he saved our land, didn't he? It's our turn to save him."

Asiri thought hard, gnawing her lower lip. It wasn't the worst idea. Cuys were ground creatures with connections to the land and the vegetation. Besides his temperament, Marco wouldn't be the worst guide.

"All right," Asiri agreed, reaching to take the sling from Tamya. "Let's go then."

"What about Ukhu Pacha?" Paqari asked.

"Yeah, that's kind of the one I'm most worried about," Paloma admitted.

Just then, they heard loud thumping noises, as if someone was pounding on a door. But the noise was coming from inside the clinic.

"I know! I know!" Asiri heard. "I know Ukhu Pacha! I know!"

Dario crossed to his office where the noise was emanating from and opened the door. With a crash, Choclo came bounding out, happy and energetic as always. She stopped to run a few circles around Dario, barking, "Hi, boy! Hi, good boy!" before darting over to Asiri.

"I know Ukhu Pacha!" she repeated to her, tail thumping hard on the ground. "I was there! Before Dario saved me."

Asiri looked at Dario, eyebrows raised high. "She says she was in Ukhu Pacha," she said hesitantly.

Dario rubbed his hand through his hair and blew out a big breath through his lips. "I don't know," he said. "She was in pretty bad shape when I found her. I wasn't sure she was going to survive.

It's possible that her spirit was between this world and Ukhu Pacha."

"Yes, yes!" Choclo confirmed, jumping up and down on her paws. "I know Ukhu Pacha! I will take you, good girl!"

"She says she'll go with me," Asiri whispered, a tear of gratitude slipping down her cheek.

With Choclo at her feet, Marco strapped to her chest and Felipe back on her shoulder, she had her three animal guides. They were not quite the sacred three, but to Asiri, they were better.

Even Marco.

"All right, now I need some dirt, any will do," Asiri said, looking around.

Paloma frowned and pointed at a potted plant. "Like that?" she asked, and Asiri nodded gratefully.

"That's perfect," she responded, removing it from the windowsill it was on. "I guess it's too much to hope that you have a bottle of alcohol stashed somewhere in your practice?" she asked Dario, as she placed it on the floor.

"I don't have any here," he admitted. "None that is drinkable, anyway." He turned hopefully to Tamya, who shook her head.

"What, you think I just hide bottles of alcohol when you're not around?" she asked defensively.

"For dioses-sake," Paqari muttered, drawing a leather flask from the small of his back. "Here," he said, thrusting it at Asiri.

"You just carry that around with you everywhere?" Paloma demanded, but he ignored her, refusing to meet her eye.

"Thank you," Asiri said quickly, not wanting them to get off track. "Now I just have to get comfortable." She folded herself onto the ground, with the plant and flask next to her.

"*I'm* not comfortable," Dario said, kneeling down next to her. "Asiri, I know that I don't know much about your life before you came to Pisqu. But this seems dangerous, and I don't want to lose you."

Asiri took his hand in hers. "Dario, I left my home and the only family I had ever known because I didn't want my path planned for me. I didn't want to live based on how other people expected me to live. I wanted to make my own decisions, and be my own person."

She could see Paloma slowly nodding behind Dario's head.

"I am doing this because I want to do this—because I *can* do this. The Amaru needs help, and I'm going to help him. I'm going to bring him back."

She leaned forward and kissed his lips softly. "And then I'm coming home to you," she whispered, quiet enough for only him. Dario kissed her again, harder this time, and then let her go. With a nod, he sat back on his heels.

"I believe in you," he said. "Come back to me."

Asiri began breathing in deeply, focusing completely on the task at hand. She made a small hole in the dirt of the potted plant, then uncorked the stopper in Paqari's flask. She poured a tiny amount into the hole, then took a sip herself. Asiri leaned her head backward against the wall behind her, closing her eyes. Then, slipping into her meditation, Asiri died.

Again.

TITI MONKEY /
TITI MONO

CHAPTER 27

ASIRI

When Asiri opened her eyes, she found herself in a barren landscape. As far as she could see, there was just gray dirt, flat and endless to her left, mountainous dunes to her right. She felt pressure against her legs and looked down, and there was Choclo in her spirit form, accompanying her.

"Where do you want to go?" she asked Asiri, her tail less animated than usual.

Asiri squinted, trying to remember. "When I saw the Amaru in my vision, he was in a place with lots of black and red rocks," she said. "There was smoke all around, and the horizon looked like the sky before a thunderstorm."

Choclo whined.

"What's wrong, girl?" Asiri asked her.

"I know a place like that," she said. "But scary things are there. They are not good boys," the puppy answered.

Asiri's lips pressed down into a thin line. "The supay, I know. I thought I saw them. But it's where I need to go."

Choclo whined again, but began walking. "This way," she said.

Together they cut through the dirt desert, the dull ground blending together to form a lumpy, desolate horizon. It all looked exactly the same to Asiri, but Choclo seemed to know where she was going.

After an eternity—or a few minutes—Choclo made a sharp left, Asiri following her.

As soon as they turned, in the space of a single blink of an eye, the surrounding tableau changed. They were no longer in a colorless wasteland, but at the foot of a large, angry volcano, spewing molten lava. Ash rained down around them both, lightly covering their spirit forms. Asiri looked beneath her feet and saw the same red and black rock from her vision.

"Good girl, Choclo," she said, much to the pup's delight. "Now we just have to find the Amaru."

She slinked forward carefully, being careful to check her surroundings for any suspicious-looking shadows. Choclo stayed glued to her side, alert and aware.

"There," Asiri said suddenly, recognizing a rock formation from her vision. She and Choclo were making their way towards it, when suddenly she froze in her tracks. There before her was the Amaru, on the same flat stones that she had seen, but the shadows in her vision were much, much closer now. They surrounded the Amaru's snake form.

The supay.

Choclo growled deep in her throat and Asiri placed a hand over her head to calm her.

"It's all right, Choclo," she said, though a trickle of fear slid down her spine. Technically, the supay shouldn't harm them. They existed only to torment the souls of evil people after their passing. But one could never fully trust demonios.

Slowly, Asiri approached the Amaru, who was swiveling his snake head back and forth, looking confused. The supay were surrounding him almost entirely, but opened up into a wide semi-circle as Asiri approached.

Asiri did her best not to look at any shadow demon directly. Their intangible, smokey forms she could handle. She wasn't sure what she would do if she stared at one and it suddenly started taking on a more solid form. Doing her best to swallow her fear, Asiri drew up her shoulders and jutted out her chin. Then, with one hand on Choclo for support, she addressed the supay.

"He is not for you," she told them, infusing her voice with as much confidence as she possibly could. Some of the supay crouched, others hissed.

"His body is not finished in Kay Pacha," she insisted. "It is not yet his time."

Some of the supay glided closer toward her, and she shivered as cold seeped from their forms.

"I will take him now," she said, stepping closer to the Amaru.

The supay began closing their circle again, seemingly facing Asiri. Choclo growled louder, her shoulders vibrating with the intensity of her anger.

"Shhh, Choclo," Asiri whispered, not lifting her hand from the pup's head.

Then, one of the supay stepped more forward than the others. It pointed a long misty hand towards the Amaru, then at Asiri, then back at the Amaru. Its wispy palm opened and closed a few times, then repeated the pointing.

The message was clear. They would give her the spirit of the Amaru ... for a trade.

Irritation burned in Asiri's chest. They had no claim to the creature! Still, it was not the worst outcome. At least they were willing to trade. But trade what? All she had on her was her clothing and her shoes.

And, she realized, her mother's necklace.

Disappointment doused her entire being, but Asiri didn't hesitate for a single moment as she reached up to unclasp the chain from her neck. She held the golden locket in her cupped hand for a quick moment, then placed a kiss on the metal, still warm from her skin.

"Here," she said, thrusting her palm towards the head supay. "I will give you this for him."

A tendril of smoke darted towards Asiri, sliding in between her fingers and lifting the necklace from her grasp. The other shadows joined the first, swirling around the golden offering until they formed a small, dark tornado, Asiri's hair fluttering wildly, strands slapping against her cheeks. Then, the whirling mists darted toward the volcano, and were gone.

Asiri let out a deep sigh of relief, and quickly crossed to the Amaru. He was much smaller in this realm, his snake form easy to pick up and drape around her shoulders.

"I'm bringing you home," she told him, smoothing a hand over his scales comfortingly. She looked down at Choclo.

"Are there any caves or streams nearby?" she asked her, and Choclo leapt forward.

"Follow me!" the chimú dog said.

Choclo lead them to a narrow stream, water boiling and hissing as it cut a path through the lava rocks. Asiri stepped into it, grateful that she did not have a body in this realm. If she did, the heat of the pacha would be unbearable.

Asiri followed the path of the stream until it reached a small mountain of the same lava stones and carefully made her way up the jagged slope. The fragmented spirit of the Amaru gently wrapped around her neck to avoid slipping, and Choclo scrambled and jumped up the path ahead of them. Finally, from one step to another, the water beneath her feet turned from trickling stream to rushing surf, and Asiri found herself on the beach at the edge of the ocean.

She looked down to thank Choclo for leading her out of Ukhu Pacha, but found that the dog was gone. Instead, she saw Marco sitting by her feet.

"Took you long enough!" the cuy grumbled. "I'm burning in the sun here! Don't think I don't know that your people eat my people! I refuse to become a roasted meal for you!"

Asiri rolled her eyes. Their spirit forms were not as susceptible to the elements as their physical ones, so she knew the cuy was just complaining to complain. She bent down to pick him up, noticing that as he was in his spirit form, his legs were perfectly well, as if they had never been broken at all.

"Do you know where the piece of the Amaru's spirit is here?" she asked him.

"He's wandered quite a bit away," Marco replied. "But I can feel him. He's somewhere that way," he said, motioning forward with his little paw.

Asiri began to walk. She walked for a long time, toward the seemingly never ending flat planes of sand. The cresting waves bathed her feet again and again, and it became hypnotic, a steady rhythm like the beating of a heart. They walked so long that Asiri lost track of time, which was always undefinable in the pachas, and began becoming disoriented. She did not know if she was walking straight, or backwards, or up, or down. There was just sand, and sand, and more sand, unceasing and interminable. All she could do was place one foot in front of the other, again and again and again. She felt like she was drifting. The only purpose of her life was to continue walking, forward and forward. Nothing mattered except putting one foot in front of the other, then again, and again.

Left foot, right foot, Asiri thought, dazed.

"Asiri," she heard in the distance.

Left foot, right foot, left foot, right, she continued.

"Asiri," the voice seemed further away, a distant sound, barely registrable as her name.

Left foot, right—

Suddenly, a sharp, needle-like pain assaulted her hand, and she felt herself thrown violently backwards. Her spirit flew through the air until it landed heavily on a stone floor. She was inside a room filled with many people, all crowded around a body on the ground.

No, not a single body, but three, she realized. *It's me,* Asiri thought, recognizing her physical body. Choclo was on her right with her head on Asiri's lap, Marco in a sling just below her breasts, and Felipe sat perched on her shoulder. They all had their eyes closed, deep in meditation.

A figure was hovering over her, on their knees, their hands over her own motionless ones. Suddenly, his face came into sharp focus. She moved her spirit form closer, frowning. She knew that face, didn't she? It was as if she was trying to recall something from her past, something from a long time ago.

The person leaned forward, bringing their mouth close to her ear.

"Asiri," it said.

Suddenly, his face came into sharp focus and Asiri suddenly knew with perfect clarity who he was.

Dario. It was Dario!

"Asiri," he whispered again, and she watched as he smoothed a strand of hair back from her body's face. "Come back to me," he said. Asiri's chest ached with the intensity of his gaze. He leaned his head towards her, his mouth close to her ear.

"I love you," she heard him whisper.

With a ferocious jolt, she was back on the beach, her heart practically beating through her chest. But she couldn't focus on Dario, or his words. She had to focus on her task in Kay Pacha, lest she get lost again. Asiri looked down at her stinging hand in shock. Several puncture wounds were visible, though they were not bleeding, as she technically couldn't bleed in the pachas. In fact, nothing should have been able to harm her spirit form physically, nothing could interact with her except—except her guides.

"Marco, did you bite me?" she asked him, outraged.

"Course I did, stupid girl! You were wandering, not focussed at all. Your spirit was about to slip off and never return!" he shouted at her. "I ought to bite you again!"

Resisting the urge to drop him, she moved her fingers out of range of his mouth. "Once was enough, thank you. But why?"

"The pain brought you back to your physical body, didn't it? I thought it would jog your memory, remind you of why we're here."

Asiri nodded, impressed. "It did, thank you."

"Well, don't make me do it again! Next time, I will pull your fingernail from your thumb! I will—"

"Wait!" Asiri interrupted, pointing down the shore. "Look!"

A few yards ahead of them was the Amaru's llama form. It was standing motionless, staring out at the sea. He didn't even move when Asiri quickened her pace to run up to him, but simply continued staring out at the water.

"Hey, friend," she said gently, placing Marco on the sand so that she could transfer the Amaru's snake spirit from her shoulders to wrap it around the llama's neck instead. As soon as the two pieces of his spirit touched, there was a flash of light and the Amaru was resting on the sand, fish tail, snake body and llama head altogether once again. She lifted him up off the floor like a baby, (a very heavy baby) and draped him around her shoulders once more.

"Let's go get your wings," she told him. She looked back down at her guide. The guinea pig huffed, then began leading her. After a few moments, they found an area with pouring rain and thunderous looking clouds.

"Damn," Asiri said. "No rainbows?"

"Oh sure, nothing Marco ever does is good enough, is it? I bring you a perfectly good option for getting to Hanan Pacha, but you throw it in my face! Why not just spit on me while you're at it? Ungrateful girl! You are the scum of the earth! The rot of the land! I spit on your name! I bite at the webbed flesh of your hand! The disrespect! The humiliation! The—"

"I'm sorry! I'm sorry!" Asiri interrupted. She wasn't sure if her head could hurt in this realm, but Marco sure was pushing her into a headache. "I appreciate your guidance."

Marco opened his mouth to reply—something horrible, no doubt—when the sky cracked overhead, and Asiri and the Amaru were swallowed up by lightning.

Lightning travel was by far Asiri's least favorite method of traversing the pachas. She knew she had no skin, no flesh, no body, but she swore she could still feel the stinging crackles of electricity, smell the singeing of her clothing. And afterward she always felt like her hair was extra staticy and frizzy, even in the corporeal world, which was of course impossible. Still, Asiri couldn't fault the speed of the travel. One moment they were in Kay Pacha, the next they were floating in Hanan Pacha.

The Amaru was still with her, but Marco was not. Instead, Felipe was there waiting for her, flitting by her face and gripping onto her sleeve, as the Amaru occupied his usual perch on her shoulder.

"We need to find his condor form," Asiri told the hummingbird, surprised at the sound of her voice. She rarely spoke in any of the pachas, and she sounded soft and distorted to her own ears, as if she was underwater instead of the endless sky.

Felipe gripped her sleeve tighter with his tiny talons and began pulling her through space. He was laughably small compared to her, but his strength in Hanan Pacha was unrivaled. He cut them through the air like a knife through butter. She passed swirling pink and purple fog, shielded her eyes from the brightness of stars. Inti was far, far away, so she didn't need to avert her gaze. His warmth barely reached them in this corner of the realm. Finally,

Asiri saw a lone figure floating softly through the air. It was the condor form of the Amaru, but he was not moving, not beating his wings. He was simply drifting aimlessly.

Asiri struggled to reach him, Felipe pulled with all his might. All the celestial bodies seemed to shrink further and further away until it left them in near darkness, but still Asiri struggled, as if swimming through the endless cosmos. If only the Amaru would fly, meet them halfway!

"Amaru!" Asiri tried to yell, but her voice came out bubbly and distorted. "Amaru!" she tried again, and this time, the noise drifted further. The Amaru still did not stir.

"Felipe, I don't know what to do!" Asiri admitted, frustration lending a sting to her voice. They were moving too slowly, and the condor spirit continued to drift further and further away.

Felipe looked at her, then toward the Amaru. With a determined shake of his feathers, he let go of her sleeve, and began flapping towards the creature.

"No!" Asiri cried out. Hanan Pacha was the most unreliable and infinite of Pachas. Without an anchor to the physical world, one could easily get lost. Felipe was there to guide her, but as he was not one of the sacred three, she was in turn an anchor for him.

"Come back, amigo!" Asiri cried out, but Felipe continued. Then, to her great surprise, Felipe started to grow. His little body looked bigger, almost the size of a dove. Then bigger still, his wings expanding outwards, until he was the size of a great eagle. He approached the condor form of the Amaru faster now, wings beating so powerfully Asiri could see ripples in the fabric of the realm. With a great big burst, he collected the condor in his grip, turning to fly back to Asiri. She could only watch in awe as they cut through the space between them until both were within arm's reach. With a blinding flash of light, Felipe reverted back to his regular form, tiny body trembling with effort. He returned to his place on her sleeve.

"I told you I was welcome in this realm," he told her, his voice equal parts exhausted and smug. Asiri leaned forward to kiss the top of his head.

"So you did, amigo, so you did," she replied reverently.

Without wasting any time, Asiri lifted the fragmented Amaru off of her shoulders and reached forward to the condor spirit. With a deafening, cosmos-crackling boom, the pieces of his fragmented spirit joined, and the Amaru flashed before their eyes, complete and whole.

He looked at Asiri, confusion making way for recognition, and with a loud bray of his llama head, he was gone.

Asiri allowed the connection between herself and the pachas to sever, and her spirit form snapped back into her human body. With a gasping inhale, she opened her eyes—

and the first thing she saw was Dario.

JAGUAR / OTORONGO

CHAPTER 28

DARIO

C hoclo bounded away from Asiri's side, and Felipe flew off of his perch on Asiri's shoulder. As carefully as he could, Dario plucked Marco from Asiri's grasp and handed him back to his sister before hauling Asiri into his arms. He buried his head in her shoulder, his own shaking with relief.

Asiri had only been meditating for half an hour, but it was the longest half an hour of his life. She had been completely immobile, and he had resisted the urge to check the rise and fall of her chest every other minute just to make sure that she was still breathing.

"Dario," she gasped, and the word was the sweetest thing that he had ever heard in his life.

"Dario," she repeated, gripping his back. "Did it work?"

He was loath to release her, but turned just in time to see the Amaru lift the upper half of his body from the exam table. The creature looked at every person in the room once, then brayed loudly. Paloma and Paqari scrambled backwards as he spread his wings and launched himself off the table, landing in front of Dario and Asiri. Dario let his grip on Asiri relax fractionally as the Amaru got closer to her.

The room was quiet as he stared into Asiri's eyes. Finally, leaning forward, he pressed his llama nose at the hollow of her throat. With a gasp, Asiri's hand flew up to clutch at her mother's necklace, which, Dario realized with a frown, hadn't been there a moment before. Then, with another loud cry, the Amaru turned to fly through the open clinic door. They all ran out to follow him just in time to see his majestic form cut across the skyline, wings completely healed and functional, beating strong and determinedly.

"Gracias," Asiri said softly, her eyes misty. "He is saying gracias."

The townspeople of Pisqu were flooding the streets, shouting and cheering, waving up at the semidios. Word of his heroics spread fast, and the people were all eager to extend their own thanks to the Amaru. Dario wrapped his arm around Asiri's shoulder, pulling her in closer to him as they watched the Amaru fly out towards the horizon, finally disappearing from sight.

"I think people will feel differently about Amarus from now on," he murmured, and watched as Asiri smiled. They looked at each other for a long moment until Asiri turned into his arms. She lifted her hands to his chest and opened her mouth to say something.

A pointed cough interrupted her. Startled, both she and Dario jumped back. Paqari was glaring at them.

"Explain. Now." he said.

Laughing, Asiri buried her head against Dario's chest, and he couldn't help but chuckle with her as he slid a hand over her silken hair.

"All right," he said, motioning towards his clinic. "Let's go inside. I'll make café."

The group settled around the main waiting room as Dario prepared the coffee. As he moved around the small space, Asiri began to explain how the two of them had found the Amaru, alone and injured by the river, and how they had decided to help him. He felt a flush creep up the back of his neck as Asiri explained how "brave" and "wonderful" he had been, creating a salve and bandaging the semidios. By the time he was passing out the coffee mugs everyone sat completely enraptured, listening to Asiri explain the magical way that the Amaru seemed to control water, and how, despite being feared in Pisqu for their curses, he had actually been very sweet and gentle.

Dario finally sat down next to Asiri, and to his delight, she placed her hand over his knee. Dario switched his coffee cup to his other hand so that he could lace his fingers through hers.

His sister noticed the action, of course, her eyes flicking down to their entwined hands, grinning like an idiot. He scowled at her.

Don't embarrass me, he glared with his eyes. Hers widened in mock innocence.

Who, me? Tamya seemed to ask. Then her expression fell.

"I can't believe you didn't tell me," she said.

"We couldn't tell anyone," Dario started, then noticed Asiri flinch. "What's wrong?" he asked her worriedly, putting down his cup. "Are you all right?"

"Yes, I'm fine, it's just ..." she looked over at Tamya. "He is being very loud."

Dario frowned, confused, until he noticed that she was not looking at Tamya at all, but at Pepe. *Marco*, he reminded himself, who was still on Tamya's lap.

"What is he saying?" he asked her eagerly, but Asiri winced.

"Um, well," she hesitated. Marco wheeked louder.

"What?" Dario asked, suddenly concerned for his cuy. "Is he all right?"

"Oh, he's fine. He's just angry that we are all here talking while he is hungry. Also, he demands that you release him. He's been demanding that since we met, actually."

"Que?" Dario cried out, shocked. He had thought the guinea pig was comfortable with him! "What is he saying *exactly?*"

Asiri hesitated again, then gave a little shrug.

"Release me at once. I will spill all your grains. I will chew through the leather of your shoes," she said in a steady voice. Dario stared at Marco in disbelief. Surely, that could not be the sweet cuy he knew!

"Animal abductor, I will flee your wretched imprisonment if it's the last thing I do," Asiri continued. "And some other stuff I would rather not repeat."

Tamya was staring down at Marco in horror, and Paloma snickered.

"I like that cuy," Paqari said, amusement on his face.

"We'll deal with this later," Dario said, grabbing Marco from his sister and walking to the back room where all the cages were. "I am trying to help you, you know," he told Marco before placing him in a pen. He added plenty of food, then shut the twine mesh door. The guinea pig grunted at him, and Dario didn't think he wanted to know what he said that time.

"Why didn't you tell me?" he heard Paloma ask as he returned to the waiting room. "About your gift?" There was no accusation in her voice, just interest.

Asiri sighed, and began explaining about Casa de Murmuros, and how they had misused her abilities.

"I couldn't be sure it wouldn't be the same here in Pisqu," she said. "Even when people don't mean to, they have their own agendas, and what starts out as innocent requests can turn into demands pretty quickly."

Dario's stomach cramped with shame. She had explained her past to him when he had found out about her gift, but it had been a fraught moment. He hadn't been able to fully process what she was trying to say. This time he really listened, and his heart broke for her when he finally realized what her life had been before coming to them.

"And, at the end of the day, I suppose I just wanted to be normal," Asiri admitted. "I wouldn't give my gift up for the world, but I wanted people to treat me the same as they would treat anyone else. I just wanted a chance at a normal life."

Paloma crossed the room to give her a big hug, and Dario saw Asiri relax. He hadn't realized how anxious she was about Paloma's reaction, but it seemed that her friend's acceptance melted the worry right off of her body.

"What happened when the Amaru fragmented? You didn't actually visit the pachas, did you?" Paqari asked her.

Dario had been wondering the same thing, but had been afraid to ask. Asiri nodded, and launched into an explanation of what had happened in Ukhu, Kay, and Hanan Pacha. Dario's blood turned cold as she spoke about meeting the supay, and nearly losing herself in Kay Pacha. Any annoyance he felt towards the guinea pig vanished when she explained how he had bitten her to bring her back to herself. Dario noticed that her eyes flickered to his, and her face burst into a flush as she explained, and he wondered if she was telling them everything. He vowed to ask her about it later.

When she explained how Felipe had saved the day in Hanan Pacha, Dario stopped everything in order to bring him a cup of sugar water.

"You're a hero," he told the colibrí. "Thank you for protecting her." Then he fished out a dried piece of meat and gave it to Choclo.

"You too," he told her, patting her head. "I'm proud that you're my dog."

"They were wonderful," Asiri said, smiling at the animals. "Even Marco, in the end. They were true guides, every bit as good as the sacred three."

Dario sat back down next to Asiri and she leaned into him with a little sigh.

"All right, well I think we've taken enough of their time," Tamya said suddenly, standing up. "We should probably get going, shouldn't we?" she asked, pointedly staring at Paloma and Paqari.

"Yes, absolutely," Paloma agreed quickly, standing as well, before dragging Paqari up with her. "I have a shop to open, after all."

"I haven't finished my café," Paqari argued, and Paloma grabbed his mug from his hand and downed the lukewarm liquid in one gulp.

"Now you have," she gasped, pulling him out the door. "Dinner later, Asiri?" she called back.

"I'll meet you at Julio's!" she answered.

"I'll be back later to help with the animals," Tamya told Dario, giving him a quick kiss on the cheek. "Bye Asiri, it was nice to officially meet you!"

And then Dario and Asiri were alone once again. Even Choclo had returned to her space in Dario's office, and Felipe was nowhere to be seen.

"So," Dario said, suddenly nervous.

"So," Asiri repeated, crossing towards him. He immediately placed his hands on her hips, dipping his forehead down to press against hers.

"I was so worried," he admitted.

"I know," she said. "I'm sorry."

Dario shook his head, tilting her chin back to look at him. "Don't be sorry. This is who you are. Your gift is incredible, just like you. I was worried, but also amazed. I am in awe of you, Asiri."

She leaned forward and kissed him softly, and Dario felt his heart shatter in his chest, only to be reassembled once again.

"I heard you, you know," she whispered. "When I was in Kay Pacha, after Marco bit me. It brought me back here, to you."

"You were here?" he asked, kissing her again because he couldn't not kiss her. She nodded, her lips grazing his with the movement.

"You told me that you loved me," she said against his mouth.

Dario swallowed hard. Panic coursed through him, a million thoughts racing through his head. He made sure to sort through them to find exactly the right words before answering.

"I did," he confessed. Dario looked into Asiri's eyes. "I do."

She smiled, and it was as brilliant as a shooting star in the night sky.

"I love you too," she told him.

Dario crushed his mouth against hers, lifting her into his arms. Her legs wrapped around his body as he placed her on top of the tall waiting room desk, kissing her desperately. She matched his pace, gripping his hair and sneaking her tongue into his mouth. With a gasp, she pulled away, framing his face in her hands.

"I want to come work with you," she said, covering his cheeks and jaw with more kisses. His hand found the curve of her hip and squeezed.

"What?" he asked, disoriented by the feel of her lips on his face and the flesh in his hand.

She giggled, moving to kiss his neck. "I want to work here," she repeated. "I want to help you take care of the animals. I can tell you what is wrong and where they're hurting and all the symptoms you can't know about." She was pulling off his shirt, and her mouth began roaming his collarbone.

"Wait, wait," Dario panted, pulling her away though it felt wrong to do so. He wanted nothing more than to continue touching her, but this was too important. "I thought that you didn't want anyone to abuse your gift?"

"You wouldn't be," Asiri said, pulling him closer to her. His erection nestled between her legs, and he groaned. How was he supposed to focus like this?

"It would be my choice. My decision. And I want to help. All my life all I have wanted to do was help, and I have the chance to do that here, with you," she said, then hesitated. "Unless, you don't want me here?"

Dario couldn't help it. He grabbed her in another searing kiss. "Of course I want you here," he said, sucking her earlobe into his mouth. She moaned and arched against him. His hand circled her waist, pressed over her breast, while his other pushed her skirt up her legs. "I always want you near me," he confessed. She clutched at him. "We make a good team," he added, before proving to both of them just how well they worked together.

"I love you," he told her when they were done, sitting on the floor with their clothes rumpled and hair disheveled. Asiri was laying half across his chest, her head over his still thundering heart.

"I love you," she said, tilting her head up to smile at him.

"When I first saw you," he said, dragging his fingers through her hair, "I thought you were a sirena."

Asiri bit her lips to hold back a laugh. "Que?" she asked.

Dario nodded. "You had just come out of the river, wet and glorious and so otherworldly that I thought you were there just to tempt me."

This time she did laugh, and every inch of his skin lit up with the sound. Then she looked at him solemnly, lifting his hand to press a kiss against his knuckles.

"I thought you were beautiful, too," she admitted shyly. "I wanted nothing more than to spend my days talking to you, hearing everything you know about animals, and telling you what I've learned, too."

Dario took a deep breath. "It sometimes felt like you didn't want to be around me," he confessed. "That I irritated you with my talking or questions."

Asiri gazed up at him, surprise etched all over her face.

"Amor, *no*," she whispered, sitting up so that their faces were mere inches apart. "If I ever acted like that, it was because the animals around us were very loud, and very distracting. If I was ever short with you, it was because of them. Not you."

Understanding hit him like lightning.

"I thought ..." he trailed off, and Asiri framed his face in her hands. "I have been consumed with thoughts of you since I moved here," she assured him.

Dario kissed her again, love and relief and wonder all threatening to make his chest burst.

"We look like we've just been through an earthquake," Dario joked when they pulled apart, trying to smooth down Asiri's hair as she laughed. He took her hand.

"You really want to work here?" he asked her hopefully. She nodded.

"I just feel bad about leaving Doña Iris on her own," she confessed. "Maybe I could still stop by a few times a week..." she nibbled on her lower week.

"Tamya," Dario realized, and Asiri frowned at him.

"Que?" she asked.

"My sister. If you work here full time, I won't need her help anymore. She can work with Doña Iris," he said. "I don't want to speak for her, of course, but Tamya does anything for work. She's not too picky. 'As long as it's interesting and it pays, I'll do it,' she says. I'm sure she'd be happy to change course for a while. She gets bored pretty easily."

Asiri grinned and leaned over to kiss him. He would never get over how wonderful it felt to have her kiss him.

"Well boss, we better get started then," she said.

"Now?" Dario complained, wrapping her back into his arms. "Not yet, let's just stay here a little while longer."

She wriggled free of his grasp and jumped up, extending her hand to help him stand.

"As much as I'd love that, we can't," she told him. "Marco is yelling from the back room ...

and threatening to set this whole place on fire."

The End

Continue reading for a sneak peek of
Paloma and the Prince of Pisqu – Pisqu Sweet and Sour Book 2
Coming 2024

PALOMA AND THE PRINCE OF PISQU

"You are, by far, the loveliest thing I have ever seen. And I have lived a long, full life full of wonderful things. I have seen the sunrise through the sun pass over Machu Picchu. I have seen the oceans swell and rage in the midst of life-ending storms. I have stood on the edge of ancient, bottomless lakes and watched shooting stars paint the heavens underneath vast and barren deserts.

You are more beautiful than all of them combined.

Having the immense pleasure of looking upon you, I feel reverent. Having the privilege of touching you ..." he trailed his fingertips up her bare arm, over her shoulder, until his thumb rested just below her clavicle.

"It's an honor beyond anything that I could ever fathom, and is certainly more than I deserve. And yet, even knowing I am not worthy of it, *of you*, the heavens could crumble to ash around my very feet and it would not stop me."

Paloma trembled

"Only you could, little bird," he said, his lips a whisper away from her own. "Tell me to stop, and I will leave."

His hands framed her face, and her breath hitched. Paloma saw the barest hint of insecurity flash behind the heat in his eyes, and he stilled.

"If you do no want me," he started, shifting backwards.

Paloma gripped the front of his shirt in desperate fistfuls.

"I have never wanted anything more," she managed to gasp out, before his mouth was on hers.

Acknowledgements

I know I already dedicated this book to my mother, but I have to thank her here again too. The only reason that I know as much about my culture and my history is because of her. Thank you Mami, for making sure I grew up with cuentos Peruanos. Also, thank you for letting me read almost all of these chapters out loud to you to get your opinion. Te queiro mucho!

Thank you to Papi and Danny too, for always reminding me how much you love my writing, and encouraging me to continue. I love you both so much.

A HUGE thanks to my beta readers, Cody, Tagg, Jessica, Abby, Rachel, Maria, and Ashley. Your thoughts, notes, and recommendations helped strengthen this book SO MUCH. I appreciate you more than I could ever say!

A big shout out to my editors as well, My'Kayle Pugh and Ashley Wessel. Thank you for continually challenging me to be better. Sorry about all the em dashes. (No i'm not.)

I also need to take a moment to thank authors Isabelle Olmo and Britton Brinkley for inviting me into their writing group! Doing writing sprints with the two of you was the only reason I was able to complete this book on time. I am so fortunate to call such wonderful and talented women my friends.

And finally, to all my wonderful, incredible, life-changing readers. Thank you for talking about this book before it was even published. Thank you for continuously hyping me up, and not allowing me to doubt myself. Thank you for your messages, your videos, your words of encouragement. I get to do what I love thanks to all of you, and I will never take it for granted. I love you all!

Printed in the USA
CPSIA information can be obtained
at www.ICGtesting.com
LVHW042019051024
792928LV00003B/183